What other authors said:

Rebels of Theta by Vickie Adair, book one of the Gods of Arth Trilogy, is a mind-blowing (and mind-touching!!) work of art, which will have you holding your breath from the first page to the last. You'll feel a bond with the peaceful Thetans and share in their joy, their suffering, and also their loss. This amazing tale of a handful of men, women, and children overcoming incredible adversity for the right to be treated as people, not savages, is truly heartwarming.

Lun Kikogne, author of *Wars of Times*

In *Rebels of Theta*, Vickie Adair delivers a great read, imaginative and fast-paced! Adair has woven a compelling story around the great question of "faith" and how tightly or loosely tied to it our evolution is. She sets up a triangle of opposing forces: the so-called gods, the liars, and the innocents. These forces wrestle with the inevitable events that accompany humanity's innate desire to evolve: political unrest, religious doubt, and war.

Kristina Mercier, author of *An Agreement with Love*

Vickie Adair has mastered the fear of a realistic future dystopian existence for human beings with her Science Fiction debut, *Rebels of Theta*. Oppression is certain. Fear is certain. The only points debatable are where trust is loyal and if your prayers can be heard in this captivating page-turning novel. You will feel the emotions of life and death as the fate of the Thetans knots your stomach until the very last sentence.

Michelle Anderson Picarella, author of *Livian*

REBELS
OF THETA

Book One of **THE GODS OF ARTH** Trilogy

Vickie Adair

3₃ʳᵈc

A Third Coast Publishers LLP Publication

REBELS OF THETA

Book One of **The Gods of Arth** Trilogy

First Edition

Copyright © 2011
Story by Vickie Adair
Cover art by Charlene Bostick

Cover design & book layout by Third Coast Publishers LLP

Published by Third Coast Publishers LLP.

ISBN: 978-0-9829498-4-9

For more information and other publications visit:
www.ThirdCoastPublishers.com

"To Robbie, who made me believe in me!"

-Vickie

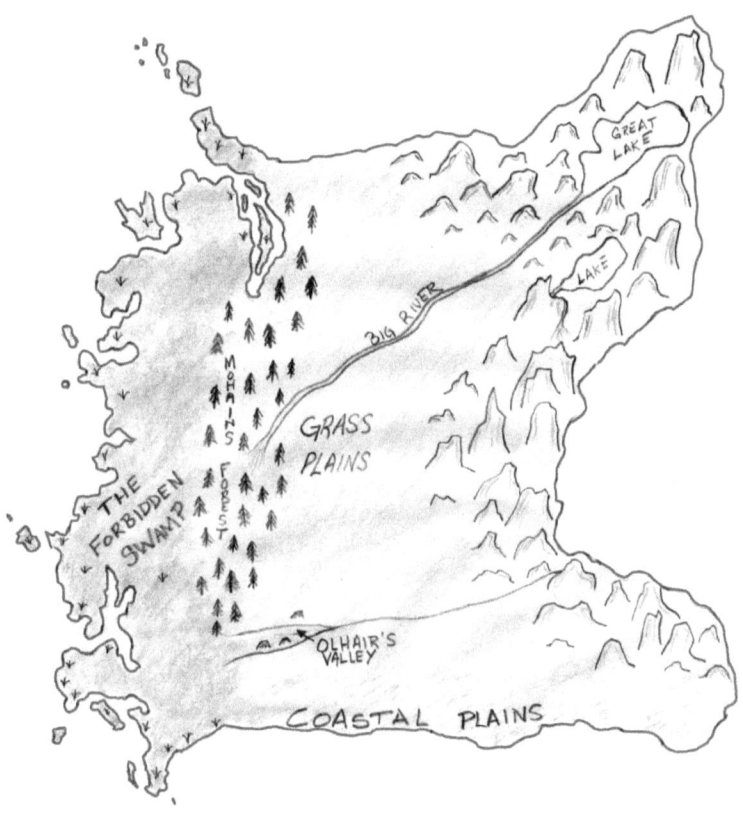

The Continent of THETA

Who first seduc'd them to that foul revolt?

John Milton, Paradise Lost

CHAPTER ONE

Kara, her muscles quivering with fatigue, sweat rolling down her body, leaned forward, until her face was against Shade's taut, ebony neck, and urged the horse on to even greater speed. The sky was still clear behind her, but she didn't know how much of a head start she had, and Shade was no match for the Seraphs' flying machines. It took all her strength now just to cling to his mane, and he was even more exhausted than she, his breath coming in ragged snorts, his powerful legs straining to carry her to safety. If she could reach Monhain Forest, she would have a chance of evading them; if not, she would die.

At the edge of Olhair's Valley, Kara raised her head to look across the valley's seemingly endless expanse of golden grass, at the distant purple haze of the forest beyond, and at the great swamp to the west, sparkling like a topaz sea beneath the setting suns. In the valley they would have no cover; Kara felt the muscles in her chest and throat constrict in fear. The horse plunged into the valley.

She reached with her mind and sensed the instinctual fear in Shade's familiar mental patterns. She mind-touched her love to the huge horse, felt the fear lessen, and then broke the connection before he could sense her concern for both their lives. But, if they died, she thought, they at least would die for a reason, unlike her mother and the others who had died since the great ships had come down from the sky. That hot summer day of her sixth year, the High-Priest and all the Disciples had gone to talk with the strangers from the sky, and when the talks had ended three days later, the Elder-Priest of each village had announced to his people that the strangers were Seraphs, messengers sent to collect offerings for the gods of Arth, gods who had commanded obedience to the Seraphs.

For the past twelve years, her people had been virtual slaves in huge grain fields, and Kara, like all her people, had accepted servitude to the Seraphs as the will of the gods. But after her mother's death, she had no longer believed the Seraphs were from the gods.

She felt bile rising in her throat from her fatigue and fear; she must survive to avenge her mother. Hoping to convince Emel and Jarta that the priests were wrong about the Seraphs, she had gone to the Seraph village and destroyed some of their strange machines. Since Marta, Emel's wife and Jarta's twin sister, had been raped by two of the Seraphs, both men had already questioned the command of obedience to the Seraphs.

Well into the valley now, she felt Shade stagger, then quickly recover.

"Only a little farther, boy," she coaxed aloud, but she doubted his strength would hold. If they could turn west into the forbidden swamp, no Seraph would follow, but, by law of the gods, no Thetan would enter the swamp either--except for Wer, but she had not seen him in over a year, not since he had been named outcast by the priests. Pushing aside futile thoughts of escape to the swamp, she concentrated on the horse that pushed himself to the limits of his endurance to save her for the second time today.

Earlier, just inside the cluster of stark gray buildings on the outskirts of the Seraph village, she had been stopped by a young red-haired Seraph, and she had reached out to Shade with her fear. The Seraph had not seen the horse coming up behind him until Shade's hooves were already descending. Her body had shaken with each blow of the hooves while Shade trampled the boy, and for one instant, she had lowered the mind-shield Thetans always maintained when around Seraphs and sensed the young Seraph's horror at his own death. She had not meant harm to anyone, only the machines. Perhaps, she thought, her Power had always been weak, limited to her mind-touch with Shade and once with Wer, because the gods had known what she would be capable of. Until today, no Thetan's Power had caused harm to another person, and the young Seraph had died like a person. His death had given her proof that the priests had been wrong.

Mid-way across the western edge of the valley, she felt the temperature dropping rapidly with the setting of the suns, and the valley turned a dusty gold in the amber twilight.

Kara was molding her body closer to Shade's for warmth when she heard the faint sound of flying machines. Over her shoulder she saw three, moving over the distant treetops like black metal bees. Her hope of escape died.

Shade, sensing her despair, ran with renewed vigor. Kara felt the strain in Shade's tired muscles, and she visualized a sharp mental image of Shade falling to his death before one of the Seraph machines killed her. Her eyes started to water at the possibility. Then, Kara heard her name echo across the valley and, without checking Shade's speed, frantically looked around for her caller.

"Kara!" The caller's voice echoed again.

There! Barely visible in the fading light, the figure of a man stood just outside the dark shape of the forbidden swamp silhouetted across the sky's first glow of suns-set. The figure waved his arms and stepped further into the valley's dim light. "Kara, here!" His voice called once more.

It was Wer!

Without even a fleeting thought for the gods' law, she signaled to Shade; the massive horse turned and lunged rapidly toward the swamp.

Stephen had been watching the girl on the magnification screen since the craft had come within visual range, and at first, all he had been able to distinguish was a small, lean female body, dressed in the scant leather attire preferred by the Thetans, masses of long black hair streaming behind her while her horse raced toward the swamp. Now as the craft came into firing range, the girl looked back, and he saw clearly her young olive-skinned face and the fear and hatred in her green eyes. Stephen shouted, "Hold your fire!"

Springing from his seat to stand and look through the hovercraft's view-plate, Stephen watched the girl disappear into the swamp.

Colonel Haley, his first officer, was making no attempt to conceal his look of scorn, and Stephen felt a blush, the curse of his fair complexion, singe his face.

"I want the girl taken alive for questioning," Stephen said. He didn't need to justify his order; he was the military commander of this planet. But the girl had committed an act of rebellion, and military retaliation should have been swift and final. "Have the other two crafts land and send out patrols to capture the girl. If your reports about the planet are correct, she can't go past the edge."

"Yes, sir," Haley replied, but the sarcasm in his voice said he thought Stephen's order had been a show of weakness, something Stephen knew he couldn't afford to show in front of his men. He was the youngest officer on the planet and, since his arrival three days ago, the youngest and most inexperienced Planetary Commander in the Federation. The men who served under him knew he had been given his command, not because he was qualified, but because he was Jason McNamara's grandson and must someday assume from the old man his birthright of Federation Premier. He knew the officers of his five-hundred-man personnel, particularly Haley, the slightly graying officer who had been in line for the position, resented his appointment almost as much as he resented it himself.

Half hoping the patrol wouldn't be able to bring in the girl, Stephen listened to Haley relay the orders. He supposed he was weak. He didn't want to interrogate and execute anyone, certainly not a young girl who couldn't possibly understand the treasonous nature of her crime. Most Thetans, kept ignorant by the agreement between the Federation and Theta's priests, had no knowledge of the Federation's claim to the planet.

Theta, the eighth and last of the home planet's colonies under the old government, had been established as a center for parapsychology research by a group of several thousand so-called telepaths and researchers. But the first supply ships for the colony had never arrived; at home, the Global Wars had begun, and on Theta, life reverted to the primitive. The books brought from home and the written records of those first abandoned settlers had been kept by their descendants, and over time, the elite group of succeeding generations who were taught to read had used those manuscripts as holy books to establish a church dictatorship.

During the Global Wars and the long years of recovery, Theta had been ignored by home. But the wars had been over for more than three hundred years, and the Federation once more traveled the galaxy to claim its own. On the first re-contact mission to Theta, the Federation delegates had dealt with the Thetan priests who had cooperated with the Federation's request for agricultural development of the planet under the conditions that the Federation not interfere with Theta's existing religion or culture and that all knowledge of the Federation and Theta's colonial history be kept from the Thetan people.

Stephen couldn't understand why his grandfather had agreed to the conditions, but he believed that the priests had sold out their own people to maintain their power. The priests were as ruthless as his grandfather. Someday, he supposed, he would be ruthless enough for leadership himself, but right now, he didn't have the stomach to kill a frightened girl, even though he was devastated by her destruction of the off-planet communications system, his one contact with home. Now he just wished he could give the order to return home, but he knew he would have to stay on this god-forsaken planet until his grandfather decided that it was time for him to leave.

Returning to the Commander's seat, he ordered sharply, "Return to base."

Stephen leaned back in his seat and prepared himself for the return to the dismal compound.

❧ · · · �֍ · · · ❦

Leaning back into the soft leather of his chair, Premier McNamara looked up from the proposal he was reading. Jackson, his secretary, crossed the large paneled office to stand in front of his antique mahogany desk.

"Excellency?" Jackson spoke calmly, but long association made McNamara aware of nervousness in his calm, efficient friend.

"Yes, Jackson."

"Sir," Jackson said, "Communications Central has been trying unsuccessfully for the past two hours to make contact with Thetan Headquarters. Central thinks the communications breakdown is permanent."

McNamara understood the nervousness. Jackson knew as well as he that the situation on Theta was unstable, and loss of communications on Theta left the boy vulnerable. Not only did Jackson love Stephen, his secretary was probably the only person who understood that he also loved his grandson. Certainly the boy had never understood.

"When is the next ship scheduled to make the Thetan run?" McNamara asked.

"Not for thirty-three days."

"Have a ship prepared to make an unscheduled jump by day after tomorrow. Make sure equipment for two complete communication systems is aboard. We should have already had back-up equipment there."

After Jackson left, McNamara went to the tinted plate glass wall. From his fiftieth floor office, he looked over the lights of the sprawling city, only recently freed from its dome, to the nearby mountain peak outlined against the black night sky. He wondered if he had made a mistake in sending Stephen to Theta. He had hoped dealing with Theta's unique problems would develop the boy's leadership skills. Stephen was his only heir to Premiership and the last of the powerful McNamara family, and he would have to be strong to finish the job Kendrick McNamara had begun almost three hundred years ago after the Global Wars had ended. All succeeding McNamaras had adhered to old Kendrick's order of priorities and had been strong enough to make the necessary decisions.

The home planet's ecology, already damaged by centuries of abuse by man, had been devastated in the Wars, and the seven colony planets had suffered major damage. Starvation and disease had been major problems, and chaos was the norm for the sixty or so surviving governments. McNamara's great-great-great grandfather, Kendrick, with a strange mixture of noble ideals and total ruthlessness, had used his position as head of the strongest of the eight surviving churches to take political control of the home planet.

Kendrick McNamara's primary objective had been saving and restoring the planet of his birth. His next objective had been preserving the colony planets. To him, individual human life and freedom were secondary to the survival of the planets. Before he turned his position over to his son, Kendrick had also gained complete control of the seven colony planets. The Federation was born. The distance to Theta made any attempt to contact possible survivors or to re-establish a colony there financially impossible during the reconstruction years, so Kendrick hadn't bothered with Theta.

And now, on the planet Kendrick ignored, there was only Stephen to succeed him, and McNamara doubted that Stephen would ever be strong enough to rule the Federation. Jason McNamara stood at the plate-glass window and watched the lights of the city slowly go out.

Watching the Quaillian women light the evening fires in front of their thatched houses, High-Priest Mathis leaned against the doorframe of the Elder-Priest's lodge. He had arrived from New Hope only moments before and was travel weary, but he continued to stand in the doorway. Squinting from the glare of the fiery suns-set, the High-Priest let his eyes wander around Quaillian, the largest settlement on Theta outside of New Hope and Visionsite with a population of just over three thousand.

The mind-shields he had sensed for the last three days, which had brought him hurrying to Quaillian, were still in place. He felt the recurring chill in his spine from sensing the shields and focused his mind to seek the villagers who were shielding from the priesthood. The people, thinking their abilities were mystic gifts from the gods, had no real understanding of their talents in telepathy, telekinetics, clairvoyance, and precognition. But at Visionsite, established by the Olhair's first order of priests for the preservation of knowledge, the psychic research begun by the first settlers continued. Mathis knew there were only a few people who possessed more than one talent and that only another strong telepath could shield from one as strong as him. It shouldn't take him long to locate the shielders.

Mathis saw Emel, his tall, muscled body as golden as his hair in the suns-set, coming into the village with his brother-in-law, Jarta. Jarta, whose normal jovial expression looked forced, carried the carcass of a goat slung across the left shoulder of his dark, stocky frame. Mathis had been worried about how these two might react ever since Emel's wife had been beaten, raped, and left damaged. Mathis reached toward them with his mind; both Emel and Jarta were shielding.

His eyes moved on to the house of Jerdon, the only renegade priest in the history of Theta and once his closest friend. Jerdon, now bedridden, lay on a cot outside his house. Mathis reached toward Jerdon, and the shield he met was like an iron wall; not one flicker of emotion escaped. He supposed, considering the animosity that now existed between them, that Jerdon would stay shielded from him anyway, but still he was bothered.

Mathis saw Lela running to meet her brother Emel and paused for a moment to admire the small blond twelve-year-old's graceful movements. Talented in both telepathy and precognition, Lela was a possible candidate for the priesthood, and Mathis was fond of her. He reached for Lela's mental pattern and was shocked to find her also shielding. She was just a child; what could she possibly have to hide?

He found a number of other villagers shielding, but the first four worried him the most; they were the most powerful paranormals of those he had found shielding. The chill in his spine intensified.

Wearily, Mathis picked up his travel bag and went into the lodge. In no mood to tolerate Mellow's fawning company, he avoided the Elder-Priest's quarters and went through the common meeting room to the guest quarters. He placed his bag on the small cot, a foot too short for his six-and-a-half foot frame and withdrew his Testament of Olhair and leather scourge from his bag. He put the book beside his bag then carried his scourge over and placed it on the washstand, the only other furnishing on the dirt floor of the windowless room. Returning to the cot, he sat down and opened the book and read, for the thousandth time, John Olhair's introduction to his testament written for the eyes of Disciples only:

"Howling wind and hard rain whipped the flap of my tent perched on Eagle Nest Mountain's rocky side. I did not hear the wind. I knelt, knees bleeding from hours on the sharp rocky ground, praying for the return of the ships from the homeworld, the world where our grandparents were born. I prayed for the survival of my people, now fewer than three thousand in number and reverting to a primitive lifestyle in their struggle with Theta IV's alien environment. The chickens and goats sent for the first settlement and twenty horses the original military commander had insisted on bringing had survived and multiplied, while the number of human survivors had diminished. I prayed, as I had for most of my forty years, that my god would send some sign that the prayers from Theta were heard across the great expanse of space that separated Theta from the homeworld.

The wind tore open the tent flap, and the driving rain swirled in and around the tent's small interior, soaking my goat skin robe, distracting me from my prayers. I was the second replacement for my god's first priest on Theta. Each of the six priests sent with the original colonists had trained a younger man to replace him before he died. I wondered then if the other gods' priests faced the same fear and doubt as I-- fear that the gods, like the homeworld, had abandoned Theta and doubt about whether the gods existed at all.

Thinking of the other priests, I received a vision of a unified church. I knew my vision was the long awaited sign come at last; I knew the destiny the gods had chosen for me. In the pouring rain, I took down my tent, eager to return to New Hope and share my vision from the gods with the other priests and lead them in uniting and worshipping gods of the homeworld in one church.

I understood then that it was the gods who had sent our people to Theta. The gods had wanted the people to return to that state of grace found only in the purity of ignorance that their ancestors had lost so long ago. The gods had revealed to me, there on the mountainside, that the people must return to a lifestyle in harmony with nature. Only a new order of priests that I and the other five priests would select and train should carry on the research the original colonists had been sent to Theta to conduct.

Unaware of the rain pelting my face, I threw my tent and gear on the land rover and started down the mountain."

Mathis closed the book and slowly removed his robes and put them on top of his bag. He went over to the washstand, his makeshift altar for the night, knelt, and prayed to the true gods that only the priests now knew. For another countless time, he prayed for guidance; had the priests' agreement with their brothers from the home planet been a mistake? For generations, the priesthood had kept the people of Theta free from the sins of their ancestors on the homeworld by keeping forbidden knowledge from them.

The early priests knew that knowledge had been the downfall of their ancestors, and they had tried to protect the people and create a new world without the sins of the old one. With their agreement with the Federation, Mathis and the other priests had hoped to keep the more than 35,000 people in the twenty-five Thetan settlements outside New Hope and Visionsite pure even after the arrival of the ship from home. But the agreement had brought only suffering to his people. Again, he prayed for help; again, he prayed for an answer; again, his prayers were answered with silence.

Reaching forward, he lifted the leather scourge from the washstand and beat his back in penitence, opening the most recent scars and creating wounds for new ones. Again, while the blood dropped from his back and soaked into the dirt floor, Mathis cried alone in the silence.

ဖ · · · ✠ · · · ❧

Wer waited for Shade to make the last great stride that would bring Kara under the cover of the outermost trees of the swamp. He had been standing just outside the cover of the swamp since the twin suns had been directly overhead, waiting to see for himself that Kara was safe.

None of his people had spoken to him since the priests had named him outcast and banished him from all the villages. But yesterday, hunting near Quaillian, he had overheard Jarta and Emel planning their own attack if Kara were successful and proved the Seraphs were not from the gods. He had been worried, for Kara and for his people.

Since the summer of his eighth year, the year the Seraphs had come, he had spent more and more of his time in the forbidden swamp. He had not listened when the priests had discovered what he was doing and forbidden him to reenter the swamps. Until the summer of his nineteenth year when he had lost his way, only Kara had known that he continued to explore the swamp. On finding his way and returning home a season later, he had been named outcast.

He had told himself it didn't matter that he was named outcast, but seeing Kara again, he knew that it had always mattered. Even when they were children, taught to use the bow and knife, to ride, and to run swiftly, when Kara was the most skillful and he was only adequate, she had been his friend, defending him when the other children laughed at his differences. Raised by Jerdon, the old physician and ex-priest, he had been different from the other children. Jerdon had taught him to read and to understand the truth of the Holy Books, a truth he had to keep secret. Secrecy had been easy; the power had been stronger in him than it had been in the other children.

The huge horse crashed into the edge of the swamp, and Kara slid off and flung her arms around his neck. His years of being different and his isolation no longer mattered. He alone on the entire planet of Theta possessed the knowledge and skills to save Kara.

How can I live without thee, how forgo
Thy sweet Converse and Love so dearly join'd
To live again in these wild Woods forlorn?

John Milton, Paradise Lost

CHAPTER TWO

Kara loosened her arms around Wer's neck, pulled back, and looked only slightly upward into his troubled brown eyes. She had never understood the magnitude of his courage until she had seen him standing there, waiting to rescue her, looking so frightfully small and alone against the great dark swamp. Tears filled her eyes now at the sight of him. He looked a little unkempt, his straight brown hair chopped off unevenly, chin length.

"Wer, how did you know?" she asked. She pushed his hair back from his face. "It doesn't matter. I just thank the gods of Arth you're here."

"And I thank the gods that the Seraphs didn't catch you. But now we should go quickly, deeper into the swamp, where we can be sure of safety."

Kara felt the slight hint of a smile, the first in months, play at her lips. "Entering the Swamp of Death has rarely been my idea of assured safety," she said. She looked ahead into the eerie swamp of gray trees that were trunks to the very top where branches covered with moss and vines made a roof over the wet world below, a different world with no sky. She shuddered, then shifted her gaze back to Wer's face.

Wer laughed and brushed his hand through her wind tangled hair before turning to lead the way into the swamp where strips of muddy ground wound through the stagnant water, and only occasionally was a patch of ground high enough to be dry. Gray stumps and large vines littered the water and ground alike, and from every direction came the frightening cries and rustling sounds of unknown animals. Kara followed fearfully.

Night brought total darkness to the gray world of the swamp, and Kara, walking as closely as possible to Wer, clutched the torch he had given her tightly enough to keep her hand from shaking. In her other hand she held the rope she led Shade by, a hand now raw and bleeding from Shade's shying at the unfamiliar sounds and scents of the swamp. But her own fear kept her from mind-touching to soothe him. Because the priests said that the Holy Books told of the evils of the swamp and the punishment of horrible deaths awaiting those who dared defy the order of the gods, she had been afraid to venture into the swamp in the day's fading light. But now, in the night, the total darkness and her own fatigue increased her fear to terror, and she fought the impulse to cling to the pack on Wer's back while they walked.

Kara knew that Wer had traveled slowly and chosen the easiest pathway for her sake, but after several hours of the aching tiredness and fear, she slowly sank to her knees in the mud, the torch falling to the dank earth before her. Her mind sank with her body into a swirling sea of darkness.

She felt Wer pulling her up and heard his voice vaguely, as if from far away. She struggled to get past the darkness, past the images floating there, giant black metal bees, the trampled body of a young red-haired boy, her mother calling out to her. She focused on Wer and on consciousness so that she could reassure him.

"I'll be fine," she said. "Just let me rest a minute."

"Come. It's not much farther to a dry place where we can sleep. Can you ride Shade?" Wer asked, handing her the torch.

"He's too tired and frightened. I can walk now."

Again they walked single file down the narrow strip of mud. Struggling to stay conscious, Kara concentrated on following Wer's back, on putting one foot in front of the other with only the light of the torches in the never-ending darkness, and on the mud always tugging at her ankles step after weary step.

At last, Wer said, "We're here," and with her next step Kara felt dry dirt under her feet. She stumbled gratefully onto the island of dryness and fell to the ground and into oblivion.

When she awoke, she saw that Wer had built a fire and now slept near her. Moving next to him, she curved her body around his back, tucked her knees into the bend of his legs, and drifted back into a world of dreams.

Later, she opened her eyes to dim gray light and carefully removed her arm from around Wer's waist, trying not to disturb him.

"I'm not asleep, Kara. I just didn't want to wake you," Wer said and rose quickly. She watched him take a bag of grain out of his pack and walk over to Shade. "It's mid-morning. We must eat and get started. If we hurry we can make it before dark to a small hunting hut I have."

She knew she should say that they should start for the edge of the swamp, knew that she had to get back to Quaillian. Last night she had simply followed, mindless from strain and fear and relief at still being alive. Now, in this strange gray place, she felt removed from the realities of yesterday. She knew she had to go back and finish what she had started--but not this minute.

"I won't slow you down today," she said.

Wer was taking dried meat and bread out of his pack. He was silent and seemed to be avoiding looking at her.

She didn't know what was bothering him, unless it was her attack on the Seraphs' village. She knew that he, like most Thetans, would be horrified at any kind of destruction. She knew he would understand when she told him what had provoked her, but she just wasn't able to talk about it yet.

Ending the silence that threatened to stretch between them, she said, "It's very dark to be mid-morning. I thought it was still early when I awoke."

Wer still did not look at her. "It's an ever dark world here," he said, his voice remote. "Sunlight doesn't reach the floor of the swamp, except in rare shafts where there is a break in the cover above."

She tried reaching to find out what emotion lay behind his behavior, but found herself no longer able to mind-touch with Wer.

"Are you angry with me, Wer?"

Instantly expressive brown eyes looked into hers, but she couldn't fathom what lay behind them. She had once known how to read every flicker that crossed his face even without the mind touch, but she had never seen the look he now gave her. Had he changed so much in a year?

"I'm not angry, Kara." He handed her a portion of the meat he had taken from his pack and broke off a piece of bread for her. "Eat now. We must leave."

For Kara, traveling through the swamp was not much easier during the day than it had been at night. The mud still sucked at their feet with each step, and Wer often led them along difficult paths, circling areas he called bottomless mud. But Shade was calmer, and Wer had bandaged her hand with leaves from a plant she had never seen, and under the leaves her hand healed rapidly. Much to Kara's relief, Wer soon seemed his old self again, explaining the mysterious world surrounding them.

Abundant animal life of both the scaled and furred varieties scurried, crawled, or slithered through the swamp, all native to the swamp and unfamiliar to Kara. At least half, according to Wer, were deadly either because they were poisonous or because they were large carnivores, like the huge lizard creatures they frequently saw moving slowly through the murky water.

The plant life was as strange and often as deadly as the animal life. Wer pointed out vines with sharp poisonous thorns and a purple flower with a sleep-inducing fragrance. Wer's talk of the swamp did little to alleviate Kara's fear. Neither talked about the Seraphs or the past or the people they both cared for.

Just after dark, they arrived at a dry area large enough for a small village. In the center sat Wer's hut, a framework of limbs covered with layers of broad, dried leaves, not much bigger than Wer himself.

Wer asked her to build a fire while he went to check his traps. When Wer returned, she cooked the unrecognizable skinned carcass he brought. She ate the unknown meat ravenously without tasting it and without asking what it was. After they had eaten, she sat absorbing the warmth of the dying fire in silent contentment, her first since her mother's death. She knew that by morning her burning hatred for the Seraphs would again drive her toward action.

"I've put hot embers in the hut," Wer said, "and there are plenty of skins. You should go and get some sleep." He stared out at the darkness that hid the surrounding dark waters and then gestured toward the fire. "I'll sleep here."

She rose slowly and brushed his cheek lightly with her lips.

"Goodnight, dear friend," she said and saw the unfamiliar expression return to his eyes.

Kara settled into the skins, and, listening to the night sounds of the swamp, the splashes in the dank waters, the haunting calls of the night birds, the chirps and cries of insects, and the running of furred nocturnal hunters, she drifted into the dreamless sleep of the exhausted.

In the gray light and dampness of the next morning, the pain that fed her hatred returned. Today, she told herself, she must tell Wer how her mother had fallen dead gathering grain for the Seraphs, how they had left her body where it had fallen until the work day ended, how her father, mad with grief, had attacked a Seraph who had beaten him on the head until he was mindless, and how her Elder-priest had come the next day and told her she must replace her mother in the fields. She must tell Wer how she had then, seeking help from Marta and Emel in the Quaillian village, fled Yorktown with Shade only to learn on her arrival that Marta had been brutally raped and beaten by two Seraphs. She must tell him how she could no longer believe the Seraphs came from the gods, how she had planned her attack on the Seraph village, and how Emel, who in his heart wanted revenge more desperately than she, had tried to talk her out of her dangerous plan, but had finally agreed to accept her success or failure as proof of whether or not the Seraphs were from the gods.

Today she would tell Wer; she knew he would understand and forgive what she had done.

When she left the hut to find him, Wer was gone. For a while she talked to Shade. Then, growing impatient waiting for Wer's return, she returned to the campfire and sat.

"Where can Wer have gone to be taking so long?" She

wondered aloud.

"They say that talking to yourself is a sign of madness."

She spun around at the sound of Wer's voice, and he held up a bundle of roots, his face a study of mock seriousness.

"Breakfast, mad-woman?"

He laughed. It sounded so good to hear laughter again that it was almost painful. Kara swallowed the lump in her throat and blinked back tears. She hated to end the laughter, but she had to tell him now while she was able to talk about it.

While Kara told her story, Wer grieved. He had loved Kara's mother; she had been as loving to him as his own mother might have been and had wept openly at his out-casting. Kara's father had been a man he admired and one who had always been kind to him. The news about Marta made his insides tighten, and he could feel his old scorn for the priests renew itself. He knew the story the priests had told about the Seraphs for the lie it was.

When she had finished, Kara sat silent for a moment, tears running down her face, and then she flung herself into his arms. Wer held her gently and rocked her while she cried. He ached to hold her tightly. Walking with her that first night in the swamp, he had felt the closeness of their lifelong friendship. And that next morning upon awakening and feeling her body beside his, he had realized that he wanted more than friendship from Kara. But the time was all wrong.

She pulled back and looked up into his face, and he reached out and held her face between his hands. "Kara, I'm so sorry. I don't know what else to say." He released her. "But, what about your father? Will he get better?"

Kara shook her head. "No. Physician Horte says that Father will be the same as long as he lives. His sister has moved him to her house to care for him."

"And Marta? Will she recover?"

"Jerdon talks with her daily, but still she remains lost in her own childhood. When I saw her, she believed me to still be the child who had played with her."

Talking about Marta was bringing Kara close to tears again, so Wer changed the subject. "And Emel?"

"As always he hides what he feels, but I know he is suffering almost unbearably. Jarta, however, spends a great deal of time with Emel, and Jarta has remained his ever optimistic self, which seems to do Emel good."

Wer chuckled. "I hadn't realized until now how I miss Jarta's loud and cheerful presence. I can remember many times being irritated to distraction by all that unfaltering happiness and goodwill. Remember in the summer festival race when I fell and broke my leg? Jarta came over and tried to cheer me up by saying that the good thing was that I hadn't been winning when I fell."

Kara smiled. "It's amazing, isn't it, how irritating cheerfulness can be if you're in a bad mood. But, when I get back, I'll be glad to see him anyway."

"When you get back?" Wer felt stunned; he couldn't lose her now. "But it's over for you now, and you'll be safe here with me."

"No. I can't stay, Wer." She pulled away from him and went to stand beside Shade. "Emel has already been talking with others who doubt the Seraphs. I can't hide here in safety and let them continue what I started."

"You could be killed." Recognizing the truth of his own words, he felt tremors run through him at the thought of her death. "Please, Kara, don't go."

"I have to go back. I want to leave today."

He thought of all the reasons he could give her for not returning and how she would reject them all. Knowing he would never be able to change her mind, Wer drew a deep breath.

"All right. As soon as we eat, we'll leave. We can make it to the forest outside Quaillian village by dark tomorrow night."

She turned away from him and buried her face in Shade's mane, and he knew she had seen his hurt.

Near dusk of the next day, they arrived where swamp merged to forest, and the ground became solid and dry beneath their feet. He knew that it must have occurred to Kara by now how useful he would be in the attempt to resist the Seraphs. She knew he had read the Holy Books, or, as he more accurately knew them, the records and books of the first settlers, and had studied the medical books and records of Jerdon. And not least, she knew his gift of the Power to be stronger than any Thetan's had ever been. He was talented in all the paranormal fields. The rebels would need his knowledge and talent, but he knew she wouldn't ask for his help. He would have to offer.

He studied her face and could see her eagerness to get on to Quaillian and her distress at having to leave him. He reached out with his mind to try and sense her emotions, but she was shielded. He smiled to himself, knowing how much Power it took to shield from him. He had always believed Kara's Power was stronger than she thought.

"How do I tell you good-bye?" she asked. And Wer knew her fear was that it would be the last good-bye, that she would not survive the rebellion against the Seraphs.

Wer turned and placed his hands on her shoulders.

"You don't say good-bye." When she started to speak, he raised a hand to silence her. "You have one small chance, the swamp; it's your only hope. Gather those foolish enough to join you in this madness and bring food, skins, and weapons, as much as you can carry. I'll start building some temporary shelters. You've only been gone two days, and it shouldn't take you more than three days to get back to the swamps edge, unless the Seraphs have taken some action against our people. I'll be here to meet you by the time the first moon has risen."

She flung her arms around him. "Oh, Wer, you'll join us?"

Gently, he pushed her away, the feel of her arms around him more than he could stand. He wanted her embrace, but not as a fellow rebel.

"Yes. Go now, and be careful until you return."

She swung herself up on Shade's back and disappeared in the growing darkness. Wer turned back into the swamp.

ᔊ · · · ✠ · · · ᔋ

In his stark gray office at the compound, Stephen listened to Haley's report on the patrol's search for the girl.

The slightly graying officer stood at ease, almost sneering. "The girl had an accomplice waiting for her; they both went into the swamp. The patrol spread out and watched for two days. They spent the last two days searching the surrounding areas and the three closest villages, but it appears the two never came out."

Stephen's fist banged the top of his desk, scattering papers. "I thought your data on this planet was accurate. I thought none of these people ventured into that damn swamp."

"Sir," Haley made the word sound like an obscenity. "We assume, since they never came out, that they chose the swamp as a form of suicide which would prevent their capture and possible betrayal of any others who might be involved."

Stephen felt the blood rush to his face. "You assume." He struggled to make his voice cold. "You assumed the girl wouldn't head for the swamp. You assumed none of these people would ever show any resistance, but you seem to have been wrong."

Haley's face turned as red as Stephen's, and the sneer on his face changed to open contempt. He made no answer.

"So far," Stephen said, "we've lost our off-planet communications system, and it'll be weeks before another ship returns. We've lost the girl, and now it seems an accomplice also. We don't know if we have two malcontents or a rebellion on our hands. I want double security at the compound maintained and a regiment sent into the swamp. If the girl is alive, I want her brought in. If she's dead, I want proof."

After a brief, almost insolent salute, Haley strode out, slamming the door behind him, and Stephen sank back in his chair. He felt drained after any confrontation with Haley, doubly so today. But he was going to have to learn to cope; he was a McNamara.

Now, all he had to do was gain the respect and loyalty of his men, get control over the people of this planet, and get control of his own turbulent emotions. He was still devastated by the loss of communication with Earth, and the sight of the girl, her hair blowing wild and free, riding across the valley had disturbed his sleep for the last two nights. Even in his waking hours, he could not keep images of the girl from intruding into his thoughts. He got up and strode to the outer office.

"Sergeant Nelson."

"Commander McNamara, sir!" The young sergeant jumped up and saluted.

At least, he thought, I get a show of respect from the lower ranks.

"Have a hovercraft readied for me. I'm going out to check preparations for the next grain shipment."

"Who would you like to pilot, sir?"

All the pilots were seasoned officers, and the last thing Stephen needed right now was to be in a subtle power struggle for the rest of the day. "I'm taking it up myself," he said. "Have it ready in half-an-hour."

Outside in the bright light of the double suns, he strolled through the compound. Built on the top of a massive plateau, the compound was strategically placed for defense, even though no one had ever thought there was any need for defense against the passive, primitive people of this planet. The gray pre-fab buildings for administration, mess, supplies, communications, and housing were scattered and had been mostly deserted during the day until recent events had proved low security unwise, but doubling security here meant pulling men from the fields and packaging plant. He went to the communications building. Looking at the damage, he could sense the girl's hatred; he should have felt anger at the destruction, but instead he felt guilty.

Two miles up in the hovercraft, flying alone, Stephen felt a peace he hadn't known since arriving on Theta. He had always loved to pilot, particularly the hovercraft, which could hover over one spot indefinitely or accelerate to a speed of two hundred miles-per-hour. Stephen looked through the view-plate at the wide expanse of planet below. Theta was a hard planet, only one large continent, tropical under the relentless heat of the two suns; the rest of the planet was one gigantic, blue-green ocean in violent turmoil from the gravitational pull of the seven moons. The gray uninhabitable swamp covered the entire western side of the continent; a tall rocky mountain range ran down the eastern side. Straight ahead, to the north, lay miles of lush, green rain forest, and east and north of the forest, were vast acres of golden grass plains where now grew two hundred thousand acres of grain. If things went according to plan, the size and production of the fields would double in less than two years.

He decelerated and began his descent to the packaging plant, saw the large, square building, gray and ugly against the surrounding fields, and felt his tension return.

"Sir!" The waiting sergeant saluted as Stephen exited the craft.

Stephen saluted. "How are things going, Sergeant?"

"Fine, sir. Although, two of our laborers didn't show today. Never happened before, but everything's on schedule."

Stephen felt a vague apprehension. "Know anything about the two missing workers?" he asked.

"We've sent two men out to talk to the priest at Quaillian to get the absent men sent in. Damned strange, though."

First, Stephen toured the inside of the plant. No Thetans were allowed inside where automated equipment moved and bagged the grain for storage until shipment. The bagged grain was running a little over minimum quota. Outside the building the Thetans unloaded the haulers as they came in from the fields, putting the grain on the conveyor belts that carried it inside the plant.

His attempts to talk to some of the workers earlier that day had been met with downcast eyes and stony silence. Always uncommunicative, the Thetans seemed to him to be unusually so today. He knew the priests had told the Thetan people that his people were some kind of angel or something; he didn't think silence would be the way to respond to an angel if you believed in that sort of thing, and his sense of apprehension grew.

He turned to the sergeant. "I'm taking the hovercraft out to the south field. Radio Sergeant Hoffmire to meet me at the landing pad," he said and headed toward the hovercraft.

Above the south field, the amber glow from the setting of the twin suns had already begun. Stephen was tired, yet his apprehension kept him from relaxing the moment the craft set down. He disembarked to find a worried looking Hoffmire standing nearer than normal to the landing pad. Hoffmire saluted.

"Any trouble here?" Stephen asked.

"You bet." Hoffmire replied, "I had twenty-seven field workers not show today. I contacted the other fields. It's the same story everywhere. In all, a hundred and ninety-two workers are missing."

"A hundred and ninety-four." Stephen replied grimly. "Two didn't show at the plant today."

"Never thought of checking with them. I sent men out to all the villages. No trace of the missing anywhere. The villagers claim they don't know where they are. Feels like trouble to me."

Stephen's apprehension became alarm. It looked like the girl's action might have been just the first action in a real rebellion.

"Go to the communications office and check back with the plant. See if the men sent from there to Quaillian learned anything. Then, contact the compound and let them know I won't be returning tonight."

That night Stephen lay sleepless in Hoffmire's quarters, piecing together the isolated incidents of the past four days into one clear picture. Hoffmire had reported just after dark that the two men sent from the plant to Quaillian had not yet returned, so maybe those men were on to something. But, Stephen was tired and lonely, and his mind kept bringing him back to the vision of the girl on the horse racing across the valley. It was with that vision that he finally drifted into sleep.

innocence, that as a veil
Had shadow'd them from knowing ill, was gone,

John Milton, Paradise Lost

CHAPTER THREE

The exhausted would-be rebels, nearly three hundred men, women, and children, wound their way through the thick brown trunks of the forest trees toward the rendezvous with Wer. Kara, forcing her legs to keep moving, was grateful that Emel had set a rapid pace, but she feared they were steadily losing ground to the two Seraphs that Jarta, rear-guard for the group, had seen tracking them for the past five hours. And now, Jarta came running up. "The Seraphs will soon catch up with us," he said.

Emel halted the group and had them cluster around him. Looking around the circle of people, many of them old friends, Kara saw women clutching their children to them, their eyes reminding her of snared rabbits. Hands gripped weapons and supply packs with whitened knuckles. Small groups huddled together in the sweltering heat as if seeking warmth. Even with her weak Power in mind-touch, Kara could sense the group's fear feeding her own. She sensed Emel's probing touch brush across the surface of her mind and felt calmer.

"The two Seraphs will be here soon" Emel said. "Either we face defeat before we begin and return at their command, or, if we are going to continue, we kill them."

"We don't even know that the Seraphs can be killed," shouted a frightened voice from the rear of the group.

"Kara has seen a Seraph die under the hooves of Shade," Emel replied. "Whatever the Seraphs may be, they die the same as men."

Kara sensed the group's increased fear at the thought of combat with the Seraphs they had always believed to be messengers from the gods. Even stronger, she felt the group's revulsion at the thought of killing. Thetans did not even kill animals unless the animal's death was necessary to provide food and clothing, and after an animal had been killed, the death was celebrated with the ceremony of everlasting life before its body was eaten. Even though many now believed the Seraphs to be demons who had deceived the priests, the deliberate killing of another living being was against all the laws they held most sacred.

"We could overpower them and leave them tied," called out a woman near the outer edge of the group. Kara heard a rumble of agreement move through the entire group.

"If we leave them alive, as soon as they free themselves or

are rescued," Emel answered, "they can pick up our trail into the swamp. We don't know how well the Seraphs can travel in the swamp, and we need all the time we can get to prepare. We will have to kill them."

Listening to Emel's words, Kara remembered the moment of horror when the young Seraph that Shade had trampled died, and she began to shake. His death had been an accident, but still horrible. The thought of deliberately taking a life appalled her. And yet she knew that to free themselves, they must all be willing to kill the Seraphs.

The Seraphs were close enough now that she could hear the hum of their land transport.

"We must kill them," Kara heard herself say.

Jerdon, his strength seeming almost rejuvenated since he was needed, rose from the lightweight litter he rode and said, "Kill them."

One-by-one, grim faced, the group began voicing their agreement. Emel nodded to Jarta. Jarta and his best friend, the tall ebony-skinned Sumar, the two best spearmen of the group, disappeared silently into the surrounding forest.

Moments later, the Seraphs' two-man transport stopped just behind the group, and the two Seraphs got out. Kara watched them start walking, unafraid, toward the group. They did not draw the weapons of the gods strapped to their sides and had only taken a few steps when the spears of Jarta and Sumar thudded into their chests. The Seraphs' faces looked bewildered as they crumpled to the ground. Mortal-red blood spread a growing stain in the dirt beneath them.

Kara heard several of the women being sick, and most of the children were crying in fear; a few of the younger children started screaming.

"Some of you come with me to hide the bodies; the more time before they're found, the older our trail is." Emel's voice broke through the noise. "Kara, take a group with you and destroy as much of the machine as possible and cover it. It will be one less they can use against us."

Kara had just signaled to a group standing near her to follow and taken a step toward the machine when she heard a strangled cry. She turned back, and the sight of Marta's face, her eyes wild with rage, her mouth drawn back in an animal snarl, made Kara freeze her steps. She watched Marta take Jarta's hunting knife from his side and run to the nearest Seraph body. Flinging herself upon the body, Marta started mutilating the corpse with frenzy.

Everyone seemed to stand frozen in horror while the knife in Marta's hand slashed with a forceful, rhythmic motion through the flesh of the dead Seraph. Then Jerdon, leaning forward, obviously trying to mind-touch with Marta to calm her, fell back holding his head with both hands, seemingly in pain from the force of Marta's insane rage.

Kara looked over at Emel, whose eyes, like windows to his soul, reflected his pain, rage, horror, confusion, and love. The curtain closed almost instantly, and there remained only the face of the calm, efficient Emel she had always known. Kara watched him gently remove the knife from Marta's blood-soaked hands, sparkling in the spotted sunlight filtering through the leaves above, raise her up, and wipe the splattered blood from her face. Holding Marta, Emel began walking once more toward the swamp. In stunned silence, the group followed. Only Kara, with Jarta and Sumar, remained to finish up.

Jarta and Sumar, with looks as dark as their blood darkened spears, smashed the inside of the machine, shattering glass, bending metal, and ripping cords. Kara, her eyes trying hard not to look at what lay beneath her, her stomach cramping, her body shaking with violent tremors, hastily gathered fallen branches and covered the bodies. All three rapidly threw branches and leaves over the damaged machine, then fled to catch up with the rest of the group.

Lela watched the two Seraphs come out of the flying machine and Elder-Priest Mellow, his round shape jiggling in effort, his babyish face glistening with sweat, hurry from his lodge to greet the Seraphs. Lela, moving casually through the almost empty village, edged closer to the spot where they would meet.

"Greetings," Mellow said. "How may I serve the Messengers of the gods today?"

"Elder Mellow," the older of the two Seraphs said, "this is Commander McNamara, our new Planetary Commander. You need to tell him anything you know about the people who are missing."

Mellow, twisting his fat little hands together, denied all knowledge of the whereabouts of the missing and said he was sure some great disaster had befallen them. In the younger Seraph's eyes, Lela saw the look of scorn for the priest who cringed before him. Lela studied the face of the tall, young Seraph. She felt the prickle of far-seeing and knew that somehow her fate was tied to the fate of this blond Seraph.

The two Seraphs left Mellow, and Lela stayed just behind them while they went from house to house questioning the villagers. When they entered her house, she slipped in behind them.

While the Seraphs stood inside the thatched walls of her house and questioned her parents about her brother Emel's disappearance, she felt contempt for her parents as they cowered before the enemy, their fear evident in their faces. She had been furious with her parents when they had refused to join Emel and the rebels making their way to the swamp.

"Please, Emel," she had pleaded with him before he left. "Take me with you."

He had picked her up and hugged her until she could no longer breathe.

"Stay here, little squirrel. You would break our parents' hearts if you came with me. Besides, we will need a spy in the villages," he had said. She knew his talk of spying had only been meant to distract her from asking to go with him, but she would show him. Hugging her again, he had said, "I love you." In silent grief, she had watched him leave the village.

Now, with the Seraphs here, she could start to play her part as spy.

Her mother reached out to pull her close, and the younger

Seraph looked directly at her with his vivid blue eyes.

"Emel is your brother, little girl?" he asked.

She hated it when anyone called her "little girl" in that patronizing tone. She gave a single nod of her head.

"What can you tell me about him?"

She spoke softly and slowly, "He is your death, Seraph." Then she turned and ran.

Outside, Lela watched for the Seraphs to leave her house. When they came out, she followed them at a distance, using all the Power acquired in her twelve years to disrupt their thought patterns with the slightest mind-touch she could manage, and still influence their mental patterns. Her crime was a double crime if she were detected by any of her own people. It was forbidden to be unshielded around the Seraphs, and it was forbidden to influence anyone's mental patterns except to aid.

As she lightly applied pressure to the young blue-eyed Seraph who strode through the village with the confidence of a young god, she was careful to keep her probing minimized, but still she picked up traces of the Seraph's personality. She felt a vague uneasiness herself. He was not a god as the priest said and not a demon as the rebels thought; in fact, his mental patterns were much like Emel's. She understood her own uneasiness, but not what her knowledge about the Seraph meant, except that the priests had lied. They must have known.

She watched the Seraphs get back into their flying machine and leave. Lela reached for Emel's familiar pattern, fearing that distance might make it impossible, but she reached him easily. She felt the joining of patterns and knew he sensed her contact, but, with no way to send words to another pattern, she could only send her confusion and not her new knowledge about the Seraphs and the priests. She also could not tell him about the faint hint in her far-seeing that the young Seraph's fate was connected to her own; she desperately wanted to talk to Emel because there had been darkness in the vision. In frustration, she broke the connection and returned to her house to begin planning a way to contact the rebels.

"We won't find out anything more at any of the other villages, Hoffmire," Stephen said, hitting the ignition button to start the hovercraft's engine for their departure from Quaillian. "I'll take you back to the south field."

He and Hoffmire had been to eleven villages before Quaillian, and, everywhere they had gone, they had received the same plea of ignorance they had received at Quaillian. When they had entered Quaillian, Stephen could sense the hostility, and the young girl's words about his death had upset him more than he wanted to admit.

About fifteen miles from Quaillian, when Hoffmire spotted a glint of metal in the forest below, Stephen put the hovercraft down, and they disembarked to investigate. Under a pile of tree limbs, just thin enough to allow sunlight to glint off the metal, a land-rover sat in a hastily made hiding place. The whole instrument panel of the craft had been smashed.

Under another mound of limbs and leaves near the craft, they found the two soldiers sent from the plant to Quaillian to talk with the priest. Both soldiers were dead--one had been mutilated.

Stephen felt his stomach start to heave. His only prior experience with death had been viewing the bodies of his parents, looking like waxed replicas, in their steel coffins. Looking at the mutilated body, Stephen experienced his first real fear of the Thetans. Hoffmire stood silent, looking the other direction, while Stephen leaned against a tree and retched.

Afterwards, he and Hoffmire loaded the bodies into the hovercraft.

Once back at the south field, Stephen helped Hoffmire unload the bodies and arranged for them to be given a burial with honors. Leaving the south field, he veered the hovercraft to the southwest to pass over the Quaillian village on his way back to the compound. It would be dark in a few minutes, or as dark as it would get tonight with the rare seven full moons, and the only thing he had accomplished today was letting Hoffmire see his weakness.

He flew low over Quaillian, and the huts glowed from the fires within like huts in any normal, peaceful village, but the two dead soldiers must have discovered something to have been killed.

South of Quaillian, towards the edge of the great swamp, the forest began to thin, and he saw the twinkling of lights, possibly torches, moving beneath the leaves. Maybe, he thought, he had stumbled onto the missing Thetans. He found a clearing large enough to land the hovercraft and walked swiftly through the moonlit forest toward where the torches had flickered toward the swamp.

He heard the horse snort before he saw them. He turned slightly and faced both horse and girl. His weapon was holstered; her bow was drawn, the arrow aimed at his chest. For a moment they remained motionless, frozen statues in the moonlight, judging each other beneath the soft rustling sound of the light breeze moving through the leaves. He was afraid, but he wasn't sure whether he was afraid of dying or was afraid of his own inability to handle Theta's problems if he didn't die. For a fleeting second, Stephen hoped she would end it for him there.

In one swift movement the girl tilted the bow, sped the arrow, spun the horse, and fled. Stephen continued staring at the vacant spot where the horse and rider had been, not even glancing down at the arrow between his boots. The girl was gone. He could feel the long distance to home, his lack of comradeship with his men, the hatred of the Thetans, and the hatred of the girl. He felt empty.

But, he knew that the missing Thetans were going into the swamp. He shook himself and buried that part of himself that belonged to the gentle woman who had been his mother. He remembered the sight of the mutilated soldier. He thought of his father, harsh and unbending, his grandfather, Jason McNamara, ruthless and powerful. He knew what he had to do.

In close recess and secret conclave sat
A thousand Demi-Gods on golden seats,

John Milton, Paradise Lost

CHAPTER FOUR

The soft soles of his boots made no sound on the granite slabs of the central courtyard as Mathis walked among Visionsite's tall stone buildings toward the chapel. The night wind from the mountaintops lifted Mathis's long gray hair and wrapped it around his eyes. His black robes, billowing in the wind made the shadow of his tall frame resemble a great night bird. But the cool wind against his skin felt warm compared to the chill he felt rising up in his soul at the thought of the coming morning. Tomorrow, he would meet with the twelve Disciple-Priests and put to the vote the two plans for stopping the destruction that faced his people.

Mathis quietly entered the stone chapel, walked up the aisle between the cold granite benches, and knelt before the great candle-lit altar. He prayed, asking the gods to guide each priest as he cast his vote. In dealing with the homeworlders twelve years ago, they had made a terrible mistake in attempting to deceive their own people; they could not afford to make another.

"Mathis," spoke a soft voice.

Mathis felt his body give a slight jump before he recognized the aging voice of Disme Hildreth, his mentor and former High-Priest.

"You startled me, Father," Mathis said, turning around to look at the stooped man whose face was deeply etched by more than ten decades of living. "I thought for once the gods had chosen to answer."

"The gods answer in their own way. Listen to your heart and follow that path. The gods will surely guide your steps through this great burden."

"And if the vote goes against me tomorrow, which path do I follow, my heart or the Disciples' decision?" Mathis asked. He looked to the old man for an answer, but Hildreth merely shook his ancient head, sending thin wisps of gray hair fluttering around his face. The old man left the chapel quietly, leaving Mathis alone with his gods.

In the morning, Visionsite sparkled and warmed in the light of the first sun's rise. So that none would guess the doubt in his heart, Mathis strode with his tall frame erect into the great meeting room. The twelve Disciple-Priests were already seated around the long wooden table when he calmly crossed the large room to take his place. Mathis looked at the faces around the table.

Chandler and Ganimard sat to the right of his chair at the head of the table; the look they returned to him assured him they would follow his lead in the vote. To their right sat Griffith, Wongson, and Lupin, each of whom averted his eyes from Mathis's glance. At the near end of table, Mathis looked down at Hsit; Hsit's steely eyes looked directly into his in challenge. Hsit meant to be High-Priest and sought any opportunity to make Mathis resign or be voted out; this vote was his chance to gain needed support from some of the Disciples.

When he reached his chair, Mathis looked down the left side of the table at the remaining six disciples. Of the six, Inskip, Jub, Dulong, Monhain, Dominicus, and Schanker, only Dominicus looked back with support.

"The meeting of the high council will come to order," Mathis said. "We will begin with presentations of the two plans for handling the rebel situation. Hsit will present his plan first."

Hsit stood, his erect six-foot-four frame towering over the seated disciples. He looked toward Mathis the way a wise parent looks toward a misbehaving child; Mathis silently gave him credit for his theatrical look. Hsit's voice was condescendingly gentle when he spoke. "Twelve years ago the disciples made a mistake in dealing with the envoy from the homeworld by not assuring that we retained absolute control of the planet. I was only an Elder-Priest at the time, and my warnings went unheeded, but it is still not too late to correct the mistakes made by that council."Hsit looked at Mathis with his last two words and paused slightly before continuing. "We must go to the homeworlders and offer to bring the rebels in and punish them ourselves. Our people can easily be convinced that the punishment is from the gods, and they will be content for a while longer to work in the fields. The offer will buy us the time we need to negotiate a new arrangement with the homeworld. Our research is our strongest bargaining tool, and with it we can convince the homeworld to leave us in charge of our own planet."

"Disciple Hsit, do you really think all the home-worlders would just go away?" Ganimard asked; the sarcasm obvious in his voice.

"No." Hsit's voice returned the sarcasm. "But if they were sure of our co-operation, they could remove all but administrative and technical personnel to handle the grain shipments and the exchange of information. The people would no longer be coming in contact with any of the homeworlders, and church control would be re-established."

"And who would supervise the labor in the fields and the packing plant?" Chandler asked.

"We would have to select the most faithful of our own people and train them to supervise," was Hsit's answer.

"That hardly seems to be in keeping with the church's purpose of equality and absence of conflict among the people," Chandler said, letting some of his scorn be heard in his voice.

"I agree," Hsit said. "But the question is no longer whether we can we adhere to our original goals of keeping the people ignorant of sin and in a state of natural grace, but whether we can salvage anything from over three hundred years of work."

There was a murmur of agreement from Hsit's supporters,

and Chandler, his eyes uneasy, looked toward Mathis. Mathis rose to bring his own large frame erect. Hsit gave a sweeping mock bow to Mathis and sat down.

"I agree with Disciple Hsit," Mathis began, "that we made a grievous error in our original agreement with the homeworld, even though I see the error somewhat differently than my fellow Priest. But my real difference of opinion with Hsit comes in the method of trying to correct our mistakes of the past. I think the time has come to tell our own people the truth. If any concealing is to be done, it should be our research that is concealed from the homeworld. Such knowledge could be an extremely destructive weapon in the wrong hands. We can ask for a grace period from the homeworld in which to explain ourselves to the people and work out some method of co-operating with the homeworlders for grain production that will be acceptable to both sides."

"Do you really expect all the people not to rebel once they hear how they were betrayed twelve years ago?" Hsit asked quietly. "We would have open warfare on our hands, and I don't doubt we would be the first victims."

"I expect a great deal of anger, Disciple Hsit," Mathis replied. "But, I have faith in the people. I think they will make the right choice."

"I suggest then that we put the question to a vote," said Hsit.

Hsit's plan was put to vote first. Mathis watched the hands slowly rise, watched hands he had counted on rising in his favor rise against him. He had expected to lose, but felt his confidence in his own plan waver when only Chandler and Ganimard voted with him. Twelve years ago, he had believed in the decisions he had helped to make; perhaps this time he had simply been wrong again.

For a while after the vote, they discussed methods and timetables for best implementing Hsit's plan. When the discussion was over, Mathis left the room with his back as straight as when he had entered.

Later, when Mathis was preparing to leave Visionsite for the homeworlders' headquarters, Disme Hildreth entered into his chamber.

"Have you made your decision?" The old man asked.

"I am on my way to meet with the new Planetary Commander," said Mathis. "I will offer to bring in the rebels and ask for thirty days in which to accomplish their capture and punishment. I am supposed to give him information about the research, but I am only going to hint that we have something more to offer than grain."

Hildreth turned and started out of the room, "May the gods have mercy on us," he mumbled.

Stephen watched the men who were installing the new planetary communications equipment with relief. He had waited the seventeen days since the old equipment had been destroyed, hoping every minute that new equipment was on the way. Now, that it was here, he dreaded contacting his grandfather with a report that would have to include the rebels and the fact that the grain shipments would be lower than expected. He knew he was over his head in dealing with an officer like Haley, but he knew that was something he would never have the courage to tell his grandfather.

The men finished installing and testing the equipment, and Stephen asked his Communications Officer to put in a request for the Premier to contact them at his convenience to receive the Thetan Planetary Report. Then he left to walk the two doors down to his office and wait tensely to be summoned to his Grandfather's return call; since his earliest memories, he had wait tensely for any coming contact with his grandfather, his only living family.

He had not even made it to his office when his Communications Officer hailed him from the doorway of the building he had just left. He turned and hurried back to sit in the communication chair, his heart pounding. He looked into the eyes of his waiting Grandfather's face and experience his normal disappointment at the lack of caring he saw in those eyes.

"Sir," Stephen said. "It's good to be in communication with you again," and realized as he spoke that it was true. He had never doubted his grandfather's strength, and, even if he had never felt loved, he had always felt his grandfather's protection.

"Commander, what happened to your Communication Equipment?" the Premier asked.

Stephen started with the attack on the Communication Building. He told his grandfather everything, except the extent of his own feelings of inadequacy to handle the situation on Theta.

Jason McNamara stared through his office's plate-glass wall to the city below shining under the mid-day sun. Only hours before he had talked with his grandson. McNamara had worried during the weeks that communications had been down, and his worst fear had now been confirmed: the situation on Theta was ready to explode. He knew it was his fault. Twelve years ago he had allowed himself to be swayed by the beauty of that undamaged planet and let a political situation, which he knew he should abolish, remain intact.

He turned back to his desk and pressed the intercom button. "Jackson," he said, "call an emergency council meeting for this afternoon. Make sure all three of the church officials will be present."

At four o'clock that afternoon, when McNamara and Jackson walked into the steel walled meeting room in the Government House basement, McNamara's military advisor and his three church officials were already seated. McNamara took his seat at the head of the stainless steel table, and Jackson took his place at the end of the table and switched on his recorder.

"Gentlemen," the Premier said, "the situation on Theta is much as I have feared during the past two weeks. The communications equipment was destroyed by a rebel, and a guard was killed. A couple of days later, two soldiers were killed by a group of rebels fleeing to the swamp. And now, there are several hundred Thetans gathering somewhere in the swamp, so further attacks are expected."

"Sir, if I may make a suggestion," said Federation

Commander Yen-Sing, head of all Federation Military Forces. "The simplest and fastest way to handle the situation is to eradicate the natives and send emigrants from our own over-crowded planet to work the fields."

McNamara looked at Yen-Sing, a small, thin man as cold and unfeeling as his cold, dark eyes. McNamara had only seen those eyes burn when Yen-Sing was able to give his troops orders to use force. McNamara didn't like Yen-Sing, but he often found him useful.

"I hope, Federation Commander, that extermination will be our last choice. For the sake of preservation of the planet, the social structure on Theta will be changed as little as possible," McNamara said. "The Thetan Church is the main problem, and the church is what we must concentrate on. Our own history has proven that the Federation government is most effective in conjunction with the True Church. However, the High-Priest came to Planetary Commander McNamara yesterday and asked for thirty days to bring in the rebels, so we have time to devise plans for bringing the Thetans into the True Church."

McNamara paused and looked around the table before continuing. "Bishop Harrold, I need a plan from you and your colleagues for undermining the faith of the Thetans in their current church and for converting them to the True Church. I want to see a written plan in two weeks."

"Yes Sir," the Bishop acknowledged.

"Federation Commander Yen-Sing," McNamara continued, "a peace keeping unit needs to be prepared for Thetan conditions and to be ready to mobilize within thirty days.

Transportation ships will need to be readied for moving Ground Forces to Theta within a day's notice."

"Do you anticipate resistance from the priests, sir?" asked Yen-Sing; there was almost a pleading sound in his voice.

"It is possible that some elements of the society will have to be eliminated. We will know more after we see the Bishop's plan at our regular session in two weeks," McNamara replied and saw Yen-Sing's dark eyes lighten at his words. "I will expect suggestions and alternate plans from all of you at that session."

Yen-Sing and his more silent colleagues saluted and left the room.

McNamara and Jackson were just outside the Premier's office before Jackson spoke. "You seem unusually troubled by the situation, Sir. We have been expecting some sort of trouble on Theta for a number of years now. Is there some development I am unaware of?"

"No," McNamara answered while Jackson opened the door to the outer office where his desk sat before the door to the Premier's private office, "just call it a gut instinct that there's something we don't know. I do occasionally have gut instincts, Jackson." McNamara smiled wryly.

"Yes, Sir," the secretary answered, "and I would trust your instincts over a thousand facts to the contrary. But I can't see what there could possibly be about Theta that we don't know."

"I don't know myself," said McNamara, "but the priests were too easy to deal with twelve years ago. I watched for some ulterior motive for a long time but never found one. Now they're offering to betray several hundred of their own people. It's not power they are after; we've slowly stripped them of any real power. And it's not greed; they've never asked us for anything and they don't take possessions from their people. The whole situation just feels wrong."

"I see what you mean, Sir," Jackson said.

McNamara wished Jackson didn't see anything; he would be less worried if this trusted friend had discounted his feelings. He stopped and turned to directly face Jackson and said, "Whatever is going on there, the next Premier of the Federation is sitting right in the middle of it."

Wer left Jerdon in his hut where the two of them had been talking for most of the morning and went to search for either Emel or Kara. The rebels had been in the swamp for over a week now, and the area was beginning to take on the appearance of a settled village. A number of permanent houses were already completed and cooking pits were already blackened.

Most of the people were busy working, building more houses, making traps, preserving food, or cooking the mid-day meal. Wer listened to the sounds around him, the construction noises, the crackle of cook fires, shouted greetings, but mostly, he listened to the sounds of laughter coming from random conversations.

He found Emel near the center of the growing village where the older children watched over the younger ones. "Emel," he said, "I've been looking for you. Jerdon and I would like to talk to you and Kara. Could you bring her to meet me at Jerdon's house?"

"Of course." Emel smiled, but Wer saw the pain beyond the smile, reached out with his mind, and sensed the intense grief Emel was feeling.

"How is Marta today?" Wer asked.

Emel turned and looked at the children playing nearby. In the midst of the group of children, Wer saw Marta laughing in total abandonment while she played chase with a group of young girls. While they stood watching Marta, Emel stood stone still, and Wer gently broke the mind-touch, leaving Emel alone with his grief.

"She's returned to a happier time," Emel finally said.

Emel turned and left; Wer looked once more at Marta, strong and beautiful, her mind lost in childhood. On his return to Jerdon's hut, Wer did not hear the laughter around him.

Wer waited with Jerdon for Kara and Emel. Seeing them approaching, he wondered how they were going to respond when they were told the truth of the Holy Books. If Kara and Emel could not cope with the truth, then the others surely could not, and the first battle would be lost before the war had begun.

As soon as Kara and Emel joined them, Wer spoke, "Before we can go any further with the rebellion, you must know the truth about our history and the Seraphs. You two must be told first and we will decide if the others are ready to hear. It won't be easy for most, and maybe not for you two, to accept the truth known to Jerdon and myself."

Giving silent consent, Kara and Emel nodded to Wer, but their eyes showed their confusion.

"The Holy Books," Wer continued, "are really records left by our ancestors of their early years on this planet. They came here on spacecraft, similar to the Seraphs' ships, from another planet to form a colony for research on what we call the power. The people on their homeworld were to keep supplies coming to the colony on a regular basis; however, the first supply shipment never arrived. Our ancestors here on Theta waited and prayed for a spaceship from home, but one never came. Having come from a highly technical world, our ancestors were ill-prepared to fend for themselves on an alien world. The number of colonist decreased rapidly while they struggled to survive on an alien planet."

Wer watched Kara's and Emel's faces as he talked, knowing they, and generations before them, had been taught by the priests that the gods had brought them from the sky to Theta.

"The first colonists' lack of survival skills is the reason the Holy Books speak so severely of the swamp; survival in such dangerous surroundings was impossible for the first settlers. They had to give more and more of their time to simple survival, and the first generation of children were taught to hunt before they were taught to read."

"By the next generation, only a few of the children, those that showed evidence of the most power, were taught to read. In that generation, parents still taught their children to pray to the god or gods their grandparents had once prayed to on the homeworld. One of the children of that second Thetan-born generation taught to read was John Olhair, the first High-Priest. The people were united by his church and waited patiently for the promised ships from their home world, Earth."

When they heard the name of their home world, Wer saw Kara and Emel both stiffened. All knew the name of the Seraph's planet, and Wer knew they had instantly made the connection.

"Twelve years ago, the long awaited ships finally returned after an absence of more than three-hundred years. The Seraphs are simply people from our home world, but they came as masters rather than brothers."

Wer looked at Kara, sitting rigid, staring out the hut door, and knew the truth had stripped her of both her history and her religion and horrified her as she realized the Seraph Wind had killed had been no more than another human like her. He looked at Emel's face and saw the same loss reflected in his steady blue eyes. Wer continued reluctantly.

"Before we can go any further with the rebellion, all of our people must understand that they fight neither servants of the gods nor demons; they fight their own people, people who share a common history and once common gods. For us to win the real war, we must learn to use the weapons and machines of our brothers, and we must teach our children to read the books of our ancestors. We will also have to let all Thetans know the truth."

Jerdon spoke for the first time since Kara and Emel had arrived. "Can you fight such a war, a war against your own people?"

Wer turned to Kara. Her hair was a tangled mess, her face looked worn, and her shoulders sagged, but he could feel his heart pounding in his throat with love when he looked at her. Slowly, she nodded her head in response to Jerdon's question.

Emel stood up and said, "Yes, we can and must fight such a war. I'm sure the others will feel the same when they hear the truth. I'll have everyone gather for a meeting in two hours."

For those rebellious, here their Prison ordain'd
In utter darkness, and their portion set
As far remov'd from God and light of Heav'n

John Milton, Paradise Lost

CHAPTER FIVE

Leaning heavily upon his staff, Jerdon feebly walked past the village fires that glowed against the blackness of the swamp night. On his way to the meeting, he faced his own doubt about the wisdom of the rebellion. He had been in his eleventh summer when he had understood the true nature of the Holy Books. Going to his old teacher with his discovery had been his first mistake in a lifetime of mistakes. When his teacher had brought him to the Disciples, they forbade him, on penalty of banishment, ever to speak of the truth again.

He had obeyed the Disciples, knowing the life he lived and

preached to be false. Jerdon, bitter by his twenties, had left the priesthood and taken up medicine, waiting for the ships from Earth to return with the truth.

He had already been old when Mathis had brought his four-year-old great-nephew, Wer, and asked Jerdon to be the boy's guardian. Mathis had been appointed Disciple the year before and had no time to care for the boy. Jerdon had taught the bright young boy the truth. Wer was to be his immortality, another generation to carry the truth and await the ships from home. But when Wer had been in his eighth summer, the ships had returned, bringing, not truth, but slavery to Theta.

Wer's banishment last year had been the final blow in a lifetime of frustrations and bitter disappointments, and Jerdon had retired to his bed to seek the relief of death. Now, the young people brought him new hope, a chance to make one final effort that would redeem him for his failure to teach the truth long ago. They also brought him new fear, fear that this time the mistakes he might make would destroy those he loved best.

Either way, he had one small part left to play in shaping Theta's future. An old observer, the time for him to lead long past, Jerdon sat down on a stump to watch the people assemble.

When the group grew quiet, Wer told them their history. In the murky darkness of the swamp, many sat stunned, robbed of gods and past. Others shouted out their need of revenge for their double betrayal by priests and Earthmen. A few spoke wisely of the obstacles before them. Then Wer told them the dangers of fighting against the Earthmen with their superior weapons, and arguments broke out over the wisdom of facing such dangers.

Emel stepped forward and raised his hands to bring order to the group. When the group was quiet, he said, "Wer and Jerdon have devised a plan for rebellion, but first we must decide if war is the course to take. We will have a show of hands by those who choose to fight."

From his stump behind the group, Jerdon watched the hands silently go up. At first only thirty or so hands were raised, but slowly, one-by-one, more hands were raised until every adult had raised a hand.

Emel stepped back and nodded to Wer.

"We have two advantages," Wer said, "the swamp and the power. To survive, you all must learn to live and travel safely in the swamp."

Jerdon listened to Wer talk about the resources and dangers of the swamp. He looked around the still group that faced Wer. Many backs were slumped, and many heads hung forward. He knew that living for an extended period of time in this sunless, damp world would be difficult for most, but at least half held their backs and heads erect, their courage visible in their bodies.

Jarta stood and asked, "What is your plan for actually fighting the Earthmen?"

"The first step," Wer said, "is to increase our forces. While we stay here in the first camp we will begin selecting a group to remain here where there is easy access to the forest. This group will be the contact for the main groups in the swamp and the outside world. The contact group left here will be responsible for getting new recruits into the swamp and gathering intelligence about the Earthmen and what is taking place outside the swamp. In a week or two the rest of us will move deeper into the swamp for safety and build three villages so everyone won't be together."

"Why can't we all stay together?" asked a woman sitting with three children near the front.

"There may be some of our own people who would betray us," Wer answered. "They may be able to locate us with the power, but they will have less of a chance if we are divided and some small groups keep moving."

"Is your plan for us to just keep running and hiding in the swamp?" shouted Jarta's friend Sumar.

"No," Wer said, "but we must have time to train. We must pool our knowledge of the Earthmen and learn all we can of their facilities and weapons. Small groups will practice making quick, forceful attacks against small groups of Earthmen and plan raids to steal some of their weapons, weapons we must learn to use. And for success, we must learn to use the Power in teams. Those gifted in mind-touch, object moving, far-seeing, and illusions must group together and turn their Powers into weapons of war."

"How will the Power help us fight?" someone asked.

"I'll give you an example," Wer answered. "If a raiding group goes out to steal weapons from the Earthmen's camp, the group will have to deal with armed guards at the camp. If our raiding group carries along several people with strong power in object moving, those with the power can move the guards' weapons at least enough to make them miss their aim."

"Do you think we'll be able to get rid of all the Earthmen on Theta?" Jarta asked.

Wer looked at Jerdon before answering. "No," he said. "The best we can hope for is to become strong enough an enemy that the government on Earth will make new agreements with us. They need the grain grown here, but we don't have to be slaves. We can work out some trade agreement where we provide grain but keep control of our own lives."

Jerdon rose from his stump and started making his way back to his hut. The meeting was ending, and on Theta a new era was beginning.

Lela, her mind shielded, walked out of the early morning light into the common meeting room where High-Priest Mathis waited. She had known and trusted him all her life, but today she thought of him as an enemy, one who had lied about the Seraphs and kept himself free while his people labored in the fields.

Two weeks ago, she had touched a Seraph's mind and learned the lie. When her eyes adjusted to the interior light, she saw the High-priest sitting on one of the hewn log benches near the front of the room.

"Thank you for coming, Lela," the High-Priest said with a fatherly expression. "I heard how distressed you were over your brother's leaving you behind."

Lela kept her face still and stared.

"Of course, your brother will be forgiven when he returns. We know he's been led astray by that old fool Jerdon and my lunatic nephew."

Watching his face closely, Lela saw that his words disturbed him almost as much as they were meant to disturb her. That old fool had been his friend once, and Wer was his dead brother's grandson. She watched Mathis's eyes focus in the direction of the swamp.

"He won't be coming back asking your forgiveness." Her voice sounded almost like the low growl of a mountain dog.

Mathis's eyes stayed focused toward the swamp, and Lela was sure now that he sought the rebels' mental patterns with his mind. Positive that the High-Priest's mind was occupied, Lela lowered her shield and carefully reached with her mind to touch his mental patterns. She sensed his feelings of guilt and knew he meant to betray the rebels.

Lela jerked her mind free and shielded. "You plan to betray them, don't you?" she asked. The High-Priest, his eyes sad, only looked at her.

"You're the traitor!" she shouted, her voice shaking with rage. She turned and ran from the priest's lodge.

Hours later, she stood in the afternoon sunshine facing the edge of the dark swamp unable to make her feet carry her forward. She had made contact with Jarta's mental pattern an hour or so earlier and sensed him drawing nearer, but time was getting short, so she could not wait for him to get to her.

Slowly, she forced one leg to make a step toward the edge of the swamp, another, and another, until the last glimpse of sunlight had disappeared from her backward glances. Her throat felt drier and tighter with each step, and at every strange sound, her heart felt as if it would pound out of her chest. She was no longer aware of her mind-touch with Jarta when he stepped into sight.

"Oh, Jarta," she cried, rushing towards his stocky body and smiling face.

When she reached him, he picked her up and asked, "Now, what brings Emel's little squirrel to the swamp?"

"I have to tell Emel about the Seraphs and the High-priest. The Seraphs are just people, just like us."

"Yes," Jarta said, "we know. Wer told us right after we came to the swamp."

Disappointed that her first news had not been news at all, Lela asked, "Do you know the priests are searching for you and plan to betray you to the Seraphs?"

"Who told you such a thing?" Jarta asked, and Lela could sense his concern.

"No one told me. High-Priest Mathis came and asked me questions about Emel, but his eyes kept focusing toward the swamp. I reached out and sensed his feelings of betrayal. I asked him. He didn't deny it."

"I must get this news to Wer," Jarta said. "I'll take you out of the swamp. There are a few hours of daylight still, so if you run, you should be able to get close to Quaillian before dark."

At the edge of the swamp, Lela made Jarta promise to give Emel her love and ask him to meet her at the swamp's edge in a week. Jarta disappeared back into the dark of the swamp. Lela stood for a few minutes looking at her brother's dark new home and shuddered. She turned and ran to the nearest patch of sunlight, threw her arms upward, looked up at the bright sky without squinting, and let the rays of the suns pour over her.

With only nine horses in the swamp, old people and children rode while the others walked on the move to the new camp. They had been traveling all day, and the suns had set an hour ago. Kara walked beside Shade who carried three of the smallest children on his broad back, and Emel and Marta followed, the last two making their way through the black night.

Jarta had caught up with them at suns-down to give Wer and Emel Lela's message. Kara felt responsible for the priests and the Earthmen knowing the rebels were in the swamp and shuddered in the darkness from the memory of her encounter near the edge of the swamp that had given them that knowledge. When she had faced the lone Seraph in the moonlight, it had been the vision of Marta, blood-drenched and blank-eyed, that had sent her arrow to the ground, an act of weakness she might well live to regret. The news that the priest sought them with the power and would betray them doubled her guilt and her fear.

At their destination, many of the first arrivals already lay sleeping around small fires. Kara's body ached to join them, but instead she went in search of Wer. She found him near one of the small fires, gently laying skins over a sleeping Jerdon.

When he saw Kara, Wer rose and followed her away from the fire.

"You're tired," he said and put an arm around her shoulder. "Why don't you try to get some sleep?"

"But, what about Lela's news? Will the priests be able to lead the Earthmen to us?"

"Don't worry. The swamp is vast and dangerous for those unfamiliar with it. We'll talk tomorrow about any changes we need to make in our plan."

After hearing that they were not all in immediate danger, Kara felt a little of the tension leave her. "I suppose, then, the sensible thing for me to do is to take your advice and go get some sleep," she said, and the smile she gave Wer was one of tired gratitude.

The next morning, Kara met with Jerdon, Emel, and Wer to discuss the new threat of the priests' betrayal.

"I think we should stay with Wer's original plan," Jerdon said. "I know some will want to react immediately to Lela's news, but hasty actions will only get some of us killed."

To Kara, Jerdon looked even frailer this morning. She knew the three day trip from the first camp had been exhausting for him, and this morning's meeting seemed to be taking an added toll on his strength. His wisdom and knowledge of the Earthmen were invaluable, and he was greatly loved by not only Wer, but by most of the Thetans. They would have to see that he took better care of himself in the future.

"Don't worry, Jerdon," Emel said softly, "the people will follow Wer's lead."

Listening to Emel, Kara thanked gods she no longer believed in that Wer had joined them. Without him and the safety of the swamp, she would have led those that followed her into an open and immediate attack.

"We need to prepare one raiding party as soon as we can," Wer said. "We must get some of the Earth weapons before making any attacks on the Earthmen."

Just as Wer finished speaking, Hamel, one of the men from the contact group, came into the camp with Elder-Priest Mellow. They headed straight to Wer, and Kara's hands clenched in both hatred and fear at the sight of the priest.

"Wer," Hamel said, "we have a new recruit. Elder-Priest Mellow came the day after Jarta left to bring you Lela's news. He has some information to add, and I thought you would want to hear it right away."

"I never thought I would do this. I never thought I would betray the priesthood," Mellow muttered as if to himself. His plump body sagged, and his normally round, rosy face was pale and creased. Then he looked directly at Wer and in a firmer voice said, "But when the High-Priest told me that two weeks ago he and the Disciples had promised the Earthmen they would capture and punish you all within a month, I couldn't be a part of it. I was afraid of how the people would react to such a betrayal."

Wer wondered how little fear it would take to send Mellow scurrying back to Quaillian, then asked, "What happens if they can't deliver?"

Mellow's face looked bewildered. "I-I don't know," he stammered.

"Then we can't take any chances," Wer said. "We'll have to make a raid for weapons in about a week. Kara, you and Emel will be in charge of the raiding party. Elder Mellow can help you plan the raid. He has been inside the Earthmen's camp."

"Yes, yes," said Mellow, rapidly nodding his round head. "I know the building they keep their weapons in."

"Well," Kara said, almost choking on her own words when she looked at the priest, "Come with me, Mellow, and give me the information about the Earthmen. Telling the truth should be a refreshing change for you."

Here Love his golden shafts employs, here lights
His constant Lamp, and waves his purple wings,

John Milton, Paradise Lost

CHAPTER SIX

Lela had been sitting in the tall grass at the edge of the swamp for three hours, waiting for Emel. She had arrived before suns-rise, hoping he would be able to meet her today. She had so much she needed to tell him. It had been a week since Jarta had carried the last message to her brother. When she saw the dark shape of her brother moving in the swamp towards her, she sprang up and waved her arms, shouting "Emel," but she did not move under the heavy foliage of the lightless swamp that she had found so frightening when she had met Jarta.

In moments, Emel, his blond hair shining in the sunslight, stood beside her. He picked her up and hugged her so tightly to his chest that she could not catch her breath.

"My little squirrel," he said still holding her, "I've missed you so much. How are you, and how are Mother and Father?"

"Fine," she said, squirming around in his arms for more breathing space. "Mother and Father both send their love, but they still refuse to join you and think you should bring Marta back to Quaillian."

Emel put her down and looked at her seriously. "I can't come home. Do you understand, little squirrel?"

"Yes, I understand. But how is Marta? Is she well yet?"

"She's not well," Emel said, and Lela hurt from the pain in his eyes, "but she's happy playing with the children of the other rebels."

Lela could think of nothing to say that would bring any comfort to her brother, so she reached out and slipped her small, slender hand into one of his large hands.

"Now," he said gruffly, "I have a mission for our top spy. I need you to tell Marta's parents that we need a disturbance that will bring most of the Seraphs to the fields or to the plant tomorrow morning. We will raid their main camp for weapons. When we get everything we can carry, we'll blow up some of their larger weapons."

Lela felt her insides growing cold at Emel's words. "You'll be careful, won't you, Emel?"

"Yes, I promise you, I'll be careful," Emel said.

"Now, do you know what the priests are planning? The

Seraphs have given them thirty days to bring us in, and they have only a week left."

"I heard that the High-Priest and all the Disciples were in New Hope, and yesterday, a man named Blade came from Visionsite to take over as Elder-Priest of Quaillian," she said, happy that Emel seemed to feel her news was important. "He held a meeting last night and said that the rebels were disobeying the gods and that the gods would punish all Thetans for what you are doing."

"How was his message received?"

"A lot of people were frightened. I think many will join the priests in trying to find you and give you to the Seraphs."

Emel merely nodded his head at the news, but Lela could see he was troubled. Gently she let her mind flow outward and link with his. She let herself feel all the strength of her love for him and was comforted by the feelings of love for her she sensed in his emotional pattern. She put her arms around him, and this time, she was the one hugging as hard as possible, her forehead near his heart.

Hurrying back to Quaillian, Lela now let fall the tears of her pain at parting which she had kept from Emel.

Stephen straightened himself behind his desk and brought his wandering mind to the matter at hand. Haley would arrive in moments for a briefing. In just over four weeks, another three hundred and forty-two Thetans had disappeared into the swamp. The month he had given the High-Priest to bring in the rebels was almost over with no sign of the original group of rebels or any who had joined them since. This morning, four workers at the plant had started shoving grain off the conveyor belts while trying to incite the others to quit working and join them. When the four had been arrested, real trouble had broken out, and Stephen had sent the extra guard company here at the compound out to the plant to get things under control.

Haley had insinuated, ever so subtly, that under his command the situation would have already been resolved. Over the past month Haley's attitude had worsened to almost open insubordination. Stephen knew he would have to be on his toes during the coming briefing.

The door slammed behind Haley after he entered the room.

"Commander," said Haley, lowering himself into a chair without permission.

Stephen studied Haley's lined face and cold, ruthless eyes. He was a good soldier, but Stephen wished the two of them were on different planets. He couldn't let the insubordination continue. He was going to have to reprimand Haley immediately. Then an explosion rocked the camp, the shock waves sliding papers across Stephen's desk, the sound temporarily deafening him.

Stephen and Haley both went through the door at a dead run, Haley just ahead. Black smoke billowed from where the main ammunition building had once stood. Several charred bodies lay visible in the smoke, and the few soldiers left of the company serving guard duty stood in shock.

As he ran toward a hovercraft, Stephen heard Haley's booming voice rising above the noise of the fire, shouting at the closest soldier, "Johnson, get some men together and get this fire out. Harris," he shouted at another soldier, "you take the rest of the men and scout the area for rebels."

Stephen knew exactly where the rebels would be heading, and he could beat them there by half-an-hour. His heart racing, he jumped in the cockpit, strapped down, and lifted-off in less than a minute. He flew low, the craft barely missing the treetops, straight to the nearest edge of the swamp. Flying up and down about a five mile stretch of the swamp's border, he watched for the rebels.

Through the sparse trees near the base of the plateau, Stephen saw about ten of them moving swiftly despite the heavy load of weapons and ammunition each carried. He aimed the craft straight towards them and fired a laser blast. As the craft, moving too fast to shift into hover-mode, passed over the rebel group, Stephen saw the man at the rear of the group fall to the ground, the upper part of his body ripped open by the beam. Then Stephen raised the nose of the craft to circle around and come back in for another shot. He would have plenty of time to get them all before they made it to the swamp.

He headed down again, this time trying to come up right behind those at the front of the group. He was almost in position to fire. He saw the girl, her hair billowing in the wind, in front of the rebels. His hand froze on the trigger of the steering column. The last thing he remembered seeing was the tree in front of the craft.

Then he heard in his dreams, "For the gods' sake, Kara,

why slow ourselves down? Just kill him now and be done with it," but he could not open his eyes to make the voices go away. He heard a girl's voice, soft and low, "Don't worry about gentleness, just strap him to two spears and drag him along as fast as possible. A prisoner we can make talk may be of more use to Jerdon and Wer than these weapons."

Then he was back on a moonlit beach, a memory from an old video file, and the breeze blew gently off the ocean. His mother with her soft voice stroked his hair and he felt warm and safe.

Later, conscious of his sore body and burning throat, he tried to ask for water, but before he could speak, he drifted back into darkness.

The sound of voices penetrated the fog in his mind.

"Kara has given us a weapon I would not have even dared pray for."

"We could have taken a prisoner at any time, Jerdon, had you told us you desired one."

"No, Emel, not a prisoner. This man is no ordinary man. He is the Planetary Commander, and if the rumor I heard on his arrival is true, not just any Planetary Commander. If the rumor is true, we now hold the grandson and heir of Earth's ruler, Premier McNamara."

Even in his delirium, Stephen recognized that he faced danger and struggled to bring his mind to full alertness. But with increased mental awareness came staggering pain.

Then he heard the same soft, low voice that brought sweet

dreams. "I would have killed him had I known. Twice now, for reasons I can't explain, I've spared this man's life."

"Kara," a new voice spoke, "I'm glad you don't find killing too easy. Besides, dead he would be no use to us."

Stephen strained to open his eyes. His vision was blurred, but he could distinguish four people standing over him. He focused on the nearest which slowly took on the distinctive features of a man, incredibly old and stooped, leaning on a staff, his alert eyes sunk deep in his face.

Stephen moved his eyes to focus on the next man, tall, blond, his face serene, but his deep blue eyes burning at Stephen with hatred. In the gentle brown eyes of the next man's young face, there was no hatred, only compassion. But, no compassion for him could be found in the large green eyes of the last face he looked into, the face that had occupied waking and sleeping moments since he had first seen it through the magnification screen. Exhausted, he lost consciousness again, and when next he opened his eyes, he looked into the soft brown eyes of his compassionate captor.

"Are you in pain?" asked the young man. "I can give you herbs to soothe pain."

Stephen closed his eyes in gratitude and relaxed in the glow of human concern. Rarely since his mother's death had he seen compassion, or, for that matter, even kindness, in any face. He felt like a sick child cradled in his mother's arms. He, having been protected all his life because of his position, felt like only half a man compared to this Thetan who survived the harshest of existences, and yet remained noble enough to offer solace to his enemy.

He felt his own long-buried needs for friendship and kindness reawakened. More than any other human he had known, he wished to call this man friend and brother. He sighed and opened his eyes once more to stare into the face of his enemy.

Stephen wanted one brief moment where they met simply as two men, not Earthman and Thetan. He strained to sit up and tell the Thetan how he admired him. Struggling to get words out, Stephen felt his body and throat rebel in agony. Finally, dictated to not by his desires, but by his damaged body, he croaked a single word, "Water," and drifted back to warm sand and gentle ocean breezes.

Jerdon woke to the smells of campfires and sizzling swamp-hog fat. The sounds of the village bustled with voices calling out in the new morning mingled with the soft calls of the swamp; he was finally growing accustomed to hearing the unfamiliar sounds each morning. There were three small villages and two lookout stations in the swamp now, but he wondered, while stretching stiff muscles to rise, what protection the swamp would have really provided against the forces at Jason McNamara's command if it had not been for yesterday's capture.

Feeling almost rejuvenated in his excitement over the capture, he left his hut and went next door to discuss new plans with Wer.

In Wer's hut, Jerdon stopped in the doorway and looked at

the scene before him. Kara paced the dirt floor and looked at Emel, her green eyes flashing confusion and anger, her lips tight. Emel remained controlled in disagreement, and Wer stood watching Kara with an insatiable hunger in his eyes.

Kara looked at Jerdon. "Jerdon," she said, "see if you can talk some sense into Emel. He can't seem to see past his own hatred to the hostage's value."

He looked into Kara's eyes when she spoke, and their minds linked. Jerdon's own emotional pattern felt assaulted from his encounter with Kara's emotional turmoil. He knew she was unaware of the true source of her emotional conflict, her own attraction to the Earthman, even now as she argued for his life. He broke free from Kara and reached out to seek Wer's pattern. Jerdon ached with the pain he sensed from Wer. He knew that Wer had understood Kara's inner conflict, and he wondered how strongly Wer would argue for the Earthman's life. "Emel?" Jerdon asked in response to Kara's plea.

"I think that we need to get rid of the prisoner, one way or another." Emel said, looking at Jerdon with defiance in his eyes, then lowered his eyes.

"We'll have to find a way to deal with our guilt, Emel, but we can't ignore the humanity of the Seraphs," Jerdon said quietly. "And this particular prisoner is far to valuable for us to get rid today."

Emel nodded once and walked out of the hut without another word.

With stunned disbelief on her face, Kara looked at him. "Do you mind explaining to me what just went on?" she asked.

"Emel has just understood that our enemies are simply men," Jerdon answered, "men who love, and fear, and laugh just like us. We are not killing monsters from another planet as most choose to believe; we are killing our own kind."

The color drained from Kara's face, her voice wavered, "I'm perfectly aware that they are men, as all of us have been since the first night in the swamp, even Emel. Why should this one Earthman upset him so much?"

Jerdon saw the pain in Wer's eyes. "He has just discovered it on a personal level with this man," he answered. "Our prisoner is the first Earthman Emel has had unshielded contact with. Why don't you just forget the incident, Kara?"

Jerdon, watching Wer stare after Kara while she disappeared from sight, wondered what problems this unforeseen emotional complication between Kara, Wer, and Stephen McNamara would bring.

Who can impair thee, mighty King, or bound
Thy Empire?

John Milton, Paradise Lost

CHAPTER SEVEN

Jason McNamara walked into the steel walled meeting room followed by his grim-faced secretary. McNamara was in no mood to humor those under his command, especially Yen-Sing. He normally practiced the good politics of letting his higher ranking officials feel they had some influence in his decision making, but today his grandson's life might rest on his decision.

Jackson sat at the end of the table and switched on his recorder. McNamara did not sit.

"Gentlemen," he said, surprised that he was having trouble controlling his voice, "the Planetary Commander of Theta has been kidnapped by the rebel group."

No one shifted in his seat. No fingers shuffled papers. Breathing was audible. Eyes met McNamara's.

"Due to the urgency of the situation," McNamara said, "whatever plans you had devised for the Thetan situation will have to be tabled. I've already made my decision. Commander McNamara's First Officer, Colonel Haley, has taken temporary command of the planet until the Commander has been rescued or returned."

Still no eyes met his, and the Premier wondered if they feared seeing a grandfather's grief and concern reflected in their Premier's eyes or if they feared seeing a Premier's calculations reflected in a grandfather's eyes.

"Commander Kay," he continued, speaking directly to his Fleet Commander, "make sure a ship large enough for three hundred is standing by to depart for Theta."

Kay nodded and McNamara looked at the Bishop. "Bishop Harrold, have a hundred parish priests and yourself ready for transport to Theta in ninety-six hours. Federation Commander Yen-Sing, you will accompany your best two hundred men for reinforcement at the Thetan base. I will be speaking with Colonel Haley on the morning of your departure to give him full details of the upcoming changes in Thetan policy and your estimated time of arrival. Yen-Sing, you and Bishop Harrold will receive detailed written orders before you depart."

Both Yen-Sing and Harrold were looking at him now. Bishop Harrold's eyes showed a rarely seen compassion. Yen-Sing's eyes glowed with anticipation.

"Are there any questions?" McNamara asked.

When no one answered or looked directly at the Premier, McNamara, his face immobile, left the now tomb-quiet room.

He took the elevator up from the Government House basement, passed the floor of his office, and continued up to his private living quarters on the fifty-first floor. Only he, Stephen, Kevin Holman, their housekeeper for the last thirty-two years, and Jackson possessed a key which would open the elevator doors on the fifty-first floor, allowing access to the entry foyer of the penthouse.

McNamara unlocked the door at the end of the foyer and stepped into the atrium. He passed through the greenery and soft flower smells, those constant reminders of what the planet had once been, to the living room, straight to the bar near the plate glass wall identical to the one in his office below. He rarely took a drink of alcohol, but today he gulped a generous shot of bourbon.

He looked out the glass to the roof tops of Albuquerque, Federation capital and the first Earth city to have its dome removed, his home, strangely empty to him now. He had not grieved much for his only son, Stephen's father. It had been Stephen's mother that McNamara had grieved for when the two had been killed in a driving accident. His son had been cold and unfeeling. He hadn't cared for this planet, its people, his own son, or even the lovely, gentle girl he had married.

Stephen was different, and now, McNamara's desire was to board the Theta bound ship himself, find Stephen and bring him home. But the Premier of eight planets could not drop things at a moment's notice to attempt a rescue of his grandson. He could only hope those he sent in his place found Stephen alive.

He heard the living room door open and turned to see Jackson.

"Are you all right, sir?" Jackson asked.

"Yes," McNamara answered, knowing as he spoke that it was true. "Were there any complaints after I left?"

"Not really. Yen-Sing, of course, is overjoyed at the prospect of having his men in combat. The Bishop may be a little disgruntled at leaving the comforts of home, his home being so comfortable," Jackson said, with an almost smile on his face. "I think the others were in a hurry to get away from me to speculate on your successor should anything happen to Stephen," he finished with no trace of a smile.

"Hostages," McNamara said confidently, "are taken to be used. If they had wanted to kill the boy, they could have. We'll just have to wait and see what their demands are. Colonel Haley will be instructed to meet whatever demands the rebels might make before reinforcements arrive, as long as the rebels can provide proof of Stephen's well-being."

"If Stephen hasn't been released by the time the ship arrives, are Yen-Sing's orders to make a rescue attempt?"

McNamara felt a touch of panic hearing Jackson's question. "No," he said, "rescue attempts always endanger the life of the hostage. If the rebels haven't already released him, I plan to let the Thetan priests bring Stephen in if they can. Then I'll destroy their church."

In the chapel of The Great Church of New Hope, Hsit's eyes blazed with fanatic light. "With Stephen McNamara's capture, the situation has changed," Mathis said as calmly as he could.

"Yes, yes," Hsit almost shouted back at him, "but it's changed to our advantage. The people believe that no one true to the church would force another person to do something against his will. We can convince the people that the rebels have turned from the gods. Their families will betray them, and the homeworlders, especially the Premier, will be doubly in debt to us."

"Would you betray your son, Hsit?" Mathis asked quietly, looking intently at the hardness of Hsit's face. "Yes," he said even more softly, "yes. I believe you would."

The sunlight coming through the lattice windows of the church made a pattern like tiny teardrops on Hsit's face. "Whether or not I would betray my son is not the issue," Hsit said.

"You're right," Mathis said, "the issue here is whether we can have the courage to reveal the truth and stop this rebellion before any more lives are lost."

"No," Hsit countered. "That issue has already been settled by vote of the Disciples, and you lost. Stephen McNamara's capture doesn't change the decision; it just provides us with the final argument we need to convince the majority of the people to turn against the rebels. The church will regain control of the planet."

"Tell me, Hsit," Mathis asked, "how will betraying your people to slave masters give the church control?"

"The Premier and his grandson will see that we can control the people and that we plan to assist them. They'll trust us to govern the planet and keep the grain shipments going. The soldiers will leave. But I don't have to argue with you. The Disciples have voted. Either support the decision or step down as High-Priest."

Looking at Hsit now, Mathis realized that Hsit did not actually believe in the gods, or the goals of the church; he only believed in power and personal gain. Mathis thought if the gods were ever going to send him the sign he so desperately prayed for, this was the time. He suddenly felt too old and tired to keep struggling on faith alone.

"I won't make it that easy for you, Hsit," Mathis said and left the chapel.

Once in the sunlit streets of New Hope, Mathis walked aimlessly through the streets of Theta's oldest settlement. The winding streets were lined with crude brick and stone buildings, many the homes of church officials, some tanning houses, trading houses, shops, and storage bins. Other buildings held technological secrets the church kept hidden from the people, the treasures left by the first colonists, old power generators, solar powered land rovers, a few still operational, and medical facilities. But Mathis did not see the streets he walked along; he was lost in his own thoughts. Hsit was right about one thing: the kidnapping would turn most of the people against the rebels. But at what cost?

He found no answers in his own thoughts.

For three hundred years the High-priest of Theta had been the most powerful man on the planet. Today, Mathis felt like a puppet whose strings were being pulled in different directions by squabbling puppet masters. He wondered briefly if Jason McNamara ever had such days.

Finally, he walked home and went directly to the altar room behind his sparse living area. After taking off his robe, he lit the altar candles and picked up his leather scourge.

Easier than Air with Air, if Spirits embrace,
Total they mix, Union of Pure with Pure
Desiring; nor restrain'd conveyance need
As Flesh to mix with Flesh, or Soul to Soul.

John Milton, Paradise Lost

CHAPTER EIGHT

Kara stood outside the small hut that housed the captive. She didn't know why she hesitated, why she felt guilty; she had every right to be here, she told herself. She had taken him captive, and somebody had to see to his needs. Having convinced herself that her only reason for coming to check on the prisoner was her responsibility as captor for the captive, Kara entered the hut.

The Seraph lay sleeping on a cot, his golden hair caked with dried blood from his head wound. Kara sat down near the head of the cot. Wer was right; there were no gods of Arth. No god would present you with the face of your enemy in such a manner as to drive all reason from your mind. She suppressed an urge to gently wipe the grime from the sleeping prisoner's face.

The Seraph moaned and shifted positions in his sleep, and Kara felt her pulse start to race. She hoped he was waking up, yet she feared he would look at her. With her fingers, she brushed her long hair away from her face. He was a Seraph; she hated the Seraphs, or Earthmen as she supposed she should call them. Just calling them the enemy might do. She wondered if while he slept he was feeling pain from his injuries.

He opened his eyes and stared at her. Self-consciously she ran her fingers through her hair again; she couldn't think of anything to say.

"How long?" he asked and closed his eyes as if exhausted by the effort of speaking. He opened his eyes again. "How long have I been here?"

"One day," Kara said. The blue eyes closed once more. "Only one day," Kara muttered to herself.

His mind too disturbed to concentrate, Emel left his morning work group trying to perfect illusions to confuse the enemy. Walking through the village, he noted that meals were cooked, children played and shrieked, mothers shouted at children, and hunters brought in game and told tales. Village life was village life be it in forest or plain or swamp.

At his own hut, Marta sat, gently rocking and softly singing to the leather doll he had made for her last week. He stood in the doorway watching her for a while before entering.

"Marta," he said, "your face is dirty and your hair is tangled. Let's get you cleaned up."

He took a cloth and wet it in the wash bowl, then gently washed the dirt from her face and hands while she squirmed and made faces at him. He took the wooden comb he had carved for her before their marriage and started combing the tangles out of her dark curls.

"Ouch," she cried and jumped away from him.

Firmly, he sat her back down and said, "Be good, Marta."

She sat like an obedient child, only flinching at his tugs on the worst tangles.

He had no gods left to pray to for her healing, but he prayed anyway, not knowing how much longer he could remain sane seeing her this way. Then a faint glimmer of hope was born. Perhaps, the obvious basic goodness of the captured Earthman might penetrate the defensive walls of her mind, but at what cost? Could he risk exposing her to the Earthman?

"Marta, come, let's go for a walk." He pulled her carefully to her feet.

Gleefully she hugged his neck. "I like to go for walks, Emel. Let's go a long way."

It was a risk he had to take.

"We will. I hope we go a long, long way today," he said.

When they entered the prisoner's small hut a few minutes later, Emel was surprised to find Kara already there, sitting beside the head of the Earthman's cot.

Wer sat in Jerdon's hut, trying to concentrate on what Jerdon was telling him about Earth's recent history and current political system, but his mind refused to stay focused on Jerdon's words. There had been no quiet moments with Kara, no gentle embraces, since she had returned to the swamp with the first group of rebels. And now, Wer thought, he had no hope of competing with the handsome young man she had taken captive.

"Now," Jerdon's voice pulled Wer out of his musings, "we must discuss what is to be done with the prisoner."

"I still don't see how he will be of use to us," Wer said, wishing his unbeatable competition were on some other world. "What can we do with him that won't bring retaliation?"

Jerdon gave Wer a troubled, penetrating look, and suddenly, Wer felt nervous. They linked, and Wer felt Jerdon's doubt and fear.

"The Power," Jerdon began, "has many possibilities, mostly forbidden."

Wer's mind reeled in shock at the implications in Jerdon's words. Was Jerdon suggesting committing the only act on

Theta that had ever been punished by death? Would he defy the most basic law of the Power and attempt to alter another's mind?

"You can't be saying we should try to change his mental patterns," Wer said, hoping to hear Jerdon confirm his statement.

"It will save a lot of lives," Jerdon grimly replied.

Wer wondered if someone had already started tampering with the Earthman's mind; he felt his insides go cold with horror. He would rather kill than rob a person of the mental patterns that made him uniquely himself. Trembling almost uncontrollably, Wer jumped up and quickly left the hut. He rushed toward the prisoner's hut, his only conscious thoughts on his need to assure himself that the prisoner was unchanged.

When he stepped through the hut door, Wer reached out for the Earthman's mental pattern with all the strength of his power, now driven by the force of all the emotional turmoil he had faced over the last few weeks. In the instant of linking, Wer's body bowed like he had received a punishing blow to the stomach, and then he fell to his knees.

In the hut, the three unguarded Thetan minds, Kara's, Emel's, and Marta's, and Stephen's vulnerable one, caught unaware by the force of Wer's intense mind-touch, locked into Wer's mental pattern--not in a mind-touch, but into something new, a total merging of five human minds.

The first mind, Marta's, lived through Stephen's memories the loneliness of duty on an alien planet and comprehended the weaknesses of those who had brutalized her. She lived Emel's pain and rage at what had been done to her, lived his grief over her illness, and loved herself through his mind. Through Kara's memory, she watched herself mutilate the dead Earthman, and forgave herself through the other four's forgiveness. She gloried at sensing her own healing, first recognized in Wer's mental pattern, then immediately known by the other four.

Emel's mind walked along the halls and into the cold metal rooms of Earth's Government House during a childhood deprived of play and laughter. He looked on the ruin that was the planet of mankind's birth; he looked on the teeming billions of humans living on the infertile planet that Stephen had seen in his life on Earth. He endured the agony of being raped and beaten, living the experience through Marta's memories. He grew stronger through sharing Marta's healing with the others. Seeing himself through four other perspectives, Emel understood his own inner strength. He could feel the others draw from his strength.

Kara saw herself, loved herself through Wer's pattern, and there understood her own love for Stephen and felt Wer's pain at the knowledge. She flew a hovercraft with Stephen's eyes and hands, buried his mother, and stood, three-feet-tall, shaking before the towering man who became her grandfather. She fell in love with the girl seen through a view plate, who was at once her and not her. She drew on Emel's calm memories of the child Kara. She hurt from being the victim of a brutalizing rape and healed with Marta.

Stephen experienced Wer's pain, loved Kara with another man's hopes and dreams, lived in the wet-scented forest, learning to throw a spear when he had barely learned to walk, and prayed to the gods of Arth. He felt his pulse race when he recalled looking down on his own sleeping face. He felt the shame of being brutalized by those thought to come from the gods and forgave himself through Marta's forgiveness for being one of a culture who brutally raped.

Wer loved himself through Kara's mind as an old friend, ached for himself because that love was nothing more, loved the tall blonde Earthman, and became the woman he loved. He admired the compassionate brown-eyed captor, himself, who looked down on his injured body and asked if he could help. He felt the surges of joy as he experienced Marta's healing through the mind of her husband. He could see himself seeing himself through four pairs of eyes.

With each person gaining and each losing something invaluable, the merging altered all five from the persons they had once been. Seeing themselves through the eyes of the others, seeing the others from their own internal perspective as well as four other perspectives, gaining knowledge, becoming citizens of multiple worlds, their minds were close to going into irreversible shock.

Wer perceived their danger, and with all the strength of the Power he possessed, struggled to break the connection. The other four, instantly in possession of Wer's concerns, assisted him, and the joining was broken.

Wer rose shakily to his feet. Emel lifted an unconscious Marta from the dirt floor. Stephen raised his eyes to look at Wer, and Kara followed his lead. Wer turned and left the hut.

Now conscience wakes despair
That slumber'd, wakes the bitter memory
Of what he was, what is, and what must be

John Milton, Paradise Lost

CHAPTER NINE

"Yes, sir," said Colonel Haley, and Premier McNamara broke the connection. Haley was sweating behind the commander's desk. The old man was tough, and Haley didn't doubt for a minute that he would be stationed on some frozen waste land of a world for the rest of his days if he didn't find the young McNamara. He thought the Premier deserved something better than that weak pup of a grandson for an heir.

Perhaps the empire would be better off if Stephen were found dead. Either way, he had already devised a plan to get the attention of the rebels in the swamp; he meant to get Stephen back before the reinforcements arrived in two weeks.

He pushed the intercom button to speak to the outer office.

"Sergeant Nelson, I want to see Major Smythe immediately."

He felt sure Major Smythe would be the man to carry out his orders. No squeamishness there. These weak Thetans would cower down fast enough when they got a taste of what Earth's military could dish out under real leadership, instead of being pampered along by some wet-nosed boy.

Minutes later, Smythe, his lean tanned face immobile, his cold gray eyes still, stood at attention.

"Major," Haley said, "the Premier wants his grandson found. The fastest way I can think of to persuade the rebels to let him go is a hostage trade-off." He watched Smythe's face for signs of reaction. "Bring in forty-eight hostages that we know have family members in the swamp, and let all the villagers know that starting in two days one hostage will be executed every two hours until young McNamara is returned. Don't be soft in choosing your hostages. Take women, children and old people along with some of their able-bodied men."

"What about priests?" Smythe asked, showing no emotion.

"No," Haley replied, "we're still under strict orders to leave the priests alone."

Smythe saluted. "I'll leave immediately, sir."

Haley watched Smythe leave the room; there had been no visible reaction from Smythe to anything he had been told. Yes, Haley thought, he had picked the right man when he had picked Smythe; he was as emotionless as the gray office walls.

He'd soon have this situation under control, and maybe

when he got young McNamara back, the old man would have the boy sent home. Haley relaxed back into the massive chair behind the commander's desk, where he knew he belonged.

~ · · · ✖ · · · ~

At each village, Smythe was met with the same confusion and disbelief, and at each, he made his announcement concerning the executions, collected the hostages he felt would most disturb the rebels, and then left for the next village. No one questioned his authority until he reached New Hope and encountered High-priest Mathis.

"I insist," the High-Priest said to him, "that you release these people until I can speak with your commander. These people you've taken aren't part of the rebellion. Why, you've taken children too young to even know what a rebellion is."

"I have my orders," Smythe answered in a bored voice.

"But to kill innocent people who have done you no harm is inhuman," the priest said, his voice barely audible.

Smythe had had all the discussion he wanted. He turned from the priest and went to the waiting cargo craft that would carry him and the twenty-two hostages already collected to the next village.

He had thirty-eight hostages by the time he reached Quaillian; he would take the last ten hostages from this village, the origin of the rebellion. The first hostage he planned to take from this village was the younger sister of a man named Emel, thought to be one of the leaders of the rebellion, at least in the first group to disappear.

He entered the house with four soldiers. One of the soldiers had to restrain the crying mother when the young blond haired girl was taken from the house. The girl did not cry; her eyes, burning with hatred, looked straight into his.

By the setting of the suns, he had his forty-eight hostages. After boarding for the return to base, he looked around the cargo hold at the odd collection of Thetans, adults both young and old with bewilderment in their faces and children crying for their parents. Only the young sister of the Quaillian Emel sat rigid, showing neither fear nor bewilderment. Smythe felt a grudging respect for the girl's courage.

The executions would begin at noon the next day.

Sitting on the cold metal floor inside the flying machine, Lela saw the speculative look the gray-eyed Seraph gave her. Briefly, she touched his mind, hoping he was too insensitive to be aware of a light probe, but, frighteningly, in her touch, she sensed no emotion at all in his mental pattern. She knew that this man would have no difficulty in carrying out the promised executions. His total lack of feeling made her stomach tighten to a cold hard lump, and she thought for a moment that she might start crying like the other children.

She was afraid and wanted to go home, wanted her mother's arms around her, and wanted her brother. In desperation, she threw all her energy into a mind-touch, straining to reach Emel in the swamp.

She made contact with Emel minutes before they landed at the Seraph's main village. Lela's stomach relaxed at his familiar touch, but when the door of the machine was opened and she was herded out with the others like cattle, Emel broke the contact.

The gray buildings of the Seraph village looked white and ghostly in the moonlight. The Thetans and their Seraph guards walked in eerie silence through the village until they were stopped by a tall man with shiny buttons on his clothes.

"Major," the new man spoke, "did you encounter any resistance gathering up the prisoners?"

The hard expression on the face of the cold-eyed man who had taken her from her house looked like a corpse's smile. "None," he said. "The rebels are the only ones on this planet with any guts."

The other man left, and the group walked on through the moonlight to a square, windowless building. Inside was a bare, gray room, too small for forty-eight people to be comfortable in, with two round seats that the Seraphs said were for body waste enclosed in the far corners.

A few hours later, Lela sat in the dark, hot, crowded room, dozing restlessly. Suddenly, she felt Emel's mind-touch, and became fully conscious. She was confused to also feel the presence of Marta, Kara, Wer, and another connecting with her mental pattern. She could not remember ever hearing of more than two patterns being able to connect at one time, and she could sense that they were reaching the other captives, too.

Images, sharp and clear, came to her. It was unlike any mind-touch she had ever experienced. The rebels were planning a rescue. She could see pictures in her mind of the rebels taking her from the Seraphs. She could feel the emotions of hope and fear coming from the other captives so strongly that they felt like a physical presence in the room.

After contact with the rebels had been broken, Lela closed her mind to the others in the room. She was frightened for the brother who would try to rescue her. Would he and those who came with him lose their own lives in a futile rescue attempt? At just after suns-rise tomorrow, she would know; either rescue would come, or her brother and friends would die before she did.

She squirmed into the most comfortable position she could find on the hard, bare floor and let her mind conjure up perhaps her last memories of the parents she had argued with so often and left behind in tears and cries of anguish. Feeling like she had suddenly been lost in a world she didn't recognize, she fell again into that uneasy sleep of one who waits for death.

In the still hours before dawn, the small blonde head lifted, and Lela stretched her muscles as much as possible without waking the small boy who lay by her, working out as much stiffness from her body as she could. Then she sat to wait the coming suns-rise, sadness like a slow twilight creeping into her soul.

Far-seeing had always been her strongest talent. Far-seeing was never sharp and clear, but now she saw no images of any tomorrows for herself. So she sat, her mind shielded, leaving fate to play the next hand.

Just beyond the last house of New Hope, Mathis stood in the early morning dark and stared toward the Seraph compound beyond his eyes' range. Earlier, he had been trying desperately to mind-touch with Lela to give her whatever comfort he could when he had sensed an extraordinary amount of psychic waves between the prisoners' mental patterns and the minds in the swamp.

He had later made a few connections with some of the prisoners, but on recognizing his pattern, they had immediately broken the connection and shielded from him. But not before he had sensed their hope. He was convinced that the prisoners hoped for rescue. What he could not understand was why. Even though there had been a great deal of psychic activity between the two groups, the mind-touch could only exchange awareness of feelings and emotional states between two people, not real communication.

If the rebels did make a rescue attempt, he would never be able to keep Hsit from meeting with Colonel Haley, and Mathis feared the outcome of such a meeting. He was quite sure that if Premier McNamara ever found out about the Power, his reactions would be far different from any Hsit envisioned.

Of course, Hsit's vision had always been distorted by his thirst for power. But if the rebels did not attempt a rescue and did not release Stephen McNamara, then forty-eight of his people were going to die.

The horizon slowly lightened with the approach of first

sun's rise. Mathis turned sharply, his dark cloak swirling after him, and strode toward the center of town. He had less than two hours until full suns-rise. He knew he hoped, maybe he prayed, that some rescue attempt was coming, but he couldn't be sure. He was sure he was going to try to make it to the base before any executions could take place.

After the roan, his fastest horse, was saddled, Mathis removed the heavy medallion of the office of High-Priest from around his neck and handed it to the young novice assigned to his household.

"Take this to Desme Hildreth," Mathis said to the novice. "He'll understand the message."

He rode at a gallop through town, feeling lighter than he had felt in ages. Once in the open, he leaned forward and spurred the horse to a run. Riding with the fierce abandonment of a youthfulness he had not known in forty years, Mathis sped through the growing light toward the rejection of his faith.

I fled, and cri'd out Death:
Hell trembl'd at the hideous Name, and sigh'd
From all her Caves, and back resounded Death.

John Milton, Paradise Lost

CHAPTER TEN

About a mile east of the Earthmen's base, thirty-four rebels led by Emel stopped just outside a small clearing. Among them were fifteen who would try to create an illusion of a battle to lure most of the soldiers from the base. The five most familiar with the Earthmen's machines would create a hauler's image in the minds of any Earthmen able to see the area where the rebels hoped to lure them. The other ten would impose on the hauler's image an image of battle. Since they could create only images and not sound, they would have to make the illusion some distance from the base.

"Give us time to reach the base before you begin," Emel said to Jarta.

"You be careful," Jarta said, "and take care of my sister."

"You mean I should take care of him, don't you?" Marta asked, shifting her large gun taken in the raid which had ended with Stephen's capture from her left shoulder to her right. "After all, I have the best weapon. During practice, my blaster blew a hole in a tree trunk."

Emel grinned at his wife, but fear turned his stomach cold. He had just got her back and now shared a type of closeness with her unlike anything he had ever even been able to imagine. He didn't want her in any danger, but he had not been able to convince her to stay behind. "I still wish you would stay here with Jarta."

"My twin," Marta said, "can make himself look like an ossap root to a wild rabbit, but I have no such talent, so I would be useless here. I can, however, handle these Earth weapons better than anyone else in the village."

Jarta laughed. "She's got you there, Emel. And I'll change my orders. Marta, take care of my brother-in-law."

A few minutes later, Emel led Marta and the other eighteen rebels trained to use the Earth weapons toward the base.

Haley rose, as was his custom, a half-hour before first suns-rise, but instead of going to breakfast as usual, he passed the mess hall and went directly to his office.

Last night, he had ordered a craft to be sent out early this morning to pick up the Elder-Priest of each village. He sent for Smythe. Haley knew he could not take any direct action against the priests, but he intended to make them watch the executions. If everything went on schedule, the first execution should take place in a few hours. Two or three executions ought to teach the fools not to rebel against Earth's policies.

Upon entering, Smythe saluted sharply and waited at stiff attention.

"Smythe, the Elder-Priests should be arriving shortly. I want everything ready for the first execution in two hours."

"Yes, sir." Smythe snapped another sharp salute and left.

When the first of the twin suns was just clearing the horizon, Haley left the command building for his overdue breakfast. A few feet from the mess door, he heard shouts from the southern end of the camp. Food forgotten, he ran toward the commotion.

Haley reached the plateau's southern edge where several soldiers directed his look past the base of the plateau. He saw flames. Smythe, already scanning the area below the plateau with his scan-bionocs, handed his bionocs to Haley.

Haley focused in on the roaring flames he had seen with his naked eye. The bionoc's distance read-out was 1.04 miles. A hauler was burning, and a handful of soldiers were under attack from a force of forty to fifty rebels. He felt his adrenaline flowing. It had been too long since he had been in a good fight.

Haley handed Smythe back his bionocs. "Will five men with blasters be enough for you to guard the prisoners with?"

"Five will be plenty," Smythe replied.

"Good. I'm taking every other soldier in camp and smashing this rag-tag group to the last man." Haley hoped the rebels had enough spunk to make the skirmish interesting.

· · · · ✖ · · · ·

At the departing of the soldiers, Lela and the other captives listened for their rescuers whose mind-touch indicated close proximity. The room was quiet, the normal shuffling and murmuring of a congregation absent. Lela felt like a dark void surrounded by living flesh, and she wanted Emel's comforting arms around her as soon as possible so she would feel real again.

Vandolph, the oldest in the group, had placed the strongest men nearby to break down the door at the first sounds of the rebels entering the base. Lela got as close to the door-breakers as possible.

The roar of the flying machines diminished to a loud hum, and then faded to silence. The group, like a single organism, braced in anticipation.

Lela felt the chill of the anticipation and remembered the childish excitement she had felt over the rebellion and the hopes she had held of playing some heroic role in the fighting. Now she only felt small and afraid. She wanted everything back the way it had been before Emel had gone to the swamp.

She tried to far-see a future day when she was safe with Emel and her parents. But she could see nothing, and then she sensed Emel's anticipation of action.

Just past the first square, gray building inside the base, Emel's group stopped, half of them guarding, half of them seeking with mind-touch to locate and count the number of soldiers left at the base.

"There are only six," Marta said, and the others who were seeking nodded in agreement.

"Five can be confused with a direct mind-touch," Marta continued, "but one has a mind that lacks imagination. He will be a serious threat."

Emel selected five of the rebel group to maintain direct mind-touch with the five soldiers whose emotional patterns they hoped to confuse. They mentally located the building which housed the prisoners near the center of the base. All six soldiers were sensed in front of the building. Emel and the rest spread out and worked their way to the building which housed the prisoners.

When everyone was in place behind the last building before the area where the soldiers stood, Emel gave the signal to attack. At the moment they charged the soldiers, firing the first round of shots, the captives within broke down the door and poured from the building. Emel, aiming with care to miss his people fleeing the building, watched his shot hit the soldier closest to him, blowing a hole the size of his fist through the man's chest. He saw two more soldiers fall to the ground at almost the same instant and his young sister Lela running with the others toward him.

Emel turned to see another soldier, with his cold, gray eyes on Marta, aiming his blaster. Emel spun to shield her from the line of fire and heard the blaster fire behind him. But the impact he expected never came. He turned back to see Lela crumpling to the ground, the blood from the wound in her shoulder already soaking her clothes. He made his first running stride toward his sister just as Marta's fire blew off the top of the gray-eyed soldier's skull.

Scooping Lela up into his arms, Emel caught a glimpse of High-Priest Mathis riding into the base as he ran for the shelter of the forest. The others, freed prisoners and rebels alike, had already begun their hasty flight down the eastern slope. He prayed for the small signs of life, the weak shuddering breath, the slow pulse visible in her neck, to continue. He held Lela tightly to his chest and ran faster than he had run in his life toward safety.

When he arrived at the clearing of the fifteen illusionists, Emel gently laid his sister's still form on the soft grass. He jerked off his shirt and wrapped it tightly around Lela's wound, trying to staunch the flow of blood.

Her eyes opened. "Emel," she spoke almost inaudibly, "tell Mother and Father that I love them."

"Tell them yourself, little squirrel," Emel's throat tightened over her nickname. He looked desperately into the fading light of her eyes.

"We're going to have this wound healed before it has time to get sore."

His tears dropped to his blood-soaked shirt.

"Make them join you. Tell them..." her voice silenced.

Lela's head rolled to one side on the sloping ground, her eyes staring sightlessly, and a small stream of blood drained slowly from her open mouth. Emel groped frantically with his mind for the familiar pattern of his sister, felt the void where her reciprocating mind-touch had once been. He gasped for breath, the pain in his chest suffocating. Lifting his dead sister, he shielded his mind against the sympathy of the others, sympathy which he would find too painful to acknowledge or accept, and started for the swamp.

Joined in creating an illusion of empty forest to prevent the Earthmen from spotting them, the others followed Emel without intruding on his grief. The whole operation had taken less than ten minutes, and there had been only one Thetan casualty.

Haley, his rage visible in each jerking step, paced in front of Smythe's sprawled body. The Thetan High-Priest stood nearby; six soldiers, morning sunshine glinting silver streaks off their weapons, stood around the priest.

Still not clear in his mind about what had happened during the last hour, Haley tried to get a mental grasp on the situation. He had led his ten hovercraft out the 1.04 miles indicated on the bionocs with the rest of his troops following in the slower land rovers. He had arrived at the designated spot in less than five minutes only to find the blaze of battle about another half-mile away. But the scene had remained illusively out of reach for another five minutes then totally vanished from sight. He had headed back to base to find the captives gone and six of his best men dead.

"I hold you responsible for this, Mathis," Haley said in a quiet, cold voice, "and I expect some answers about exactly how this rebel operation was carried out."

"I arrived on the scene only minutes before you, Colonel," Mathis said, looking him calmly in the eye, "but it seems that apparently the rebels created a diversion to draw you away and released the innocent people you planned to execute."

"They will find their effort sadly futile," Haley said, knowing his anger was driving him to danger of court-martial. "Twenty of your Elder-Priests arrived ten minutes ago. Tomorrow after our own burials have been attended to, we will begin the executions, starting with the priests." Haley had the satisfaction of seeing the color blanch from Mathis's face. "But, what I want to know is how the rebels' diversion, as you called it, was accomplished."

"No more than I," Mathis said quietly.

That night more than three-thousand Thetans crept from their homes. Using the skills of the Power and generations of hunting knowledge, they evaded guards and slipped unnoticed through the forest to disappear into the swamp.

Revenge, at first though sweet,
Bitter erelong back on itself recoils;

John Milton, Paradise Lost

CHAPTER ELEVEN

Marta, her sweat-soaked hair in dark ringlets around her face, walked in silence behind Emel and the pale still body he carried. She listened to the soft and now familiar sounds of the sunless swamp and kept her mind shielded from the sorrow surrounding her. Her sanity too recently returned to her, too fragile, to cope with Lela's death and Emel's anguish, she turned her thoughts to the pressing problems which had been created by the unusual mind-meld that had occurred between herself, Emel, Kara, Wer, and the Earthman, Stephen.

Since that day, none of them had been completely free of the other four; even now, she could feel Emel's pain though they both were shielded. But, what worried her most about their lack of freedom from each other was Kara's pain and Stephen's shame concerning Wer. Not only had Marta felt Kara's pain, she had seen the shadow that passed over Kara's eyes each time Wer was near. Wer's understanding and forgiveness could be felt by the other four, a forgiveness that, in the face of the emptiness in his heart, made them more uncomfortable than comforted. She and Emel found the personal emotions of the other three distressing; the other rebels in the swamp found the high level of emotions they sensed awkward at the least. But, for Kara, Stephen, and Wer, the situation was fast becoming unbearable. She could feel the three of them now, sensed their awareness of Lela's death.

"Marta," Jarta said. Marta stared blankly at Jarta's concerned face. "Should I try to take Lela from him? He's about to drop from fatigue."

She looked at her husband's tall, straight back now drooping slightly from the weight he carried and shook her head. "No, Jarta. He won't give her up. Don't worry."

Jarta nodded sadly, and they continued on the muddy path twisting through the stark gray tree trunks.

Kara, waiting with the pain she felt from mind-touching with the rescue group, had thought she was prepared, but, when Emel stepped into the village, the first sight of Lela's lifeless body jerked her body back like a kick in the chest from Shade. She turned and fled for the protection of her hut. She had no comfort for Emel, only her own guilt for

Lela's death.

She was no longer the young, headstrong huntress she had been on that day when she set out on her first attack against the Seraphs, and she was now facing her responsibility for starting this rebellion, a rebellion in which children were already dying.

She wondered how Stephen could love her, a savage by his standards, in light of the fate she had brought not only on her own people but on him also. Because the mind-meld had made the sensitivity and kindness he had always suppressed dominant in his personality, he would never be able to find happiness now in the life he had been raised and trained for. Yet, return to that life he must, or more innocent people would die.

Kara grew cold at the thought of Stephen's leaving. She could not lose him; she wanted to go with him. But how could she go and live among her enemies after leading her people into war against them? Perhaps, if she were able to send information back to the rebels, she could live with her decision to abandon the rebels and live with the enemy. Her fight would be from within the enemy camp. But could Stephen betray his own people? Could he live with someone who spied upon them? Would the conflict he would face, both internally and externally, erode his love for her?

Once she had carried her questions and worries to Wer, the friend who had held and comforted her for the loss of her parents. But now any confidences could only bring more hurt for them both. She swept the long tangles of black hair back from her face. What was lost could be grieved for, but never regained.

She knew she must go to Emel; his grief was pushing into the edges of her mind even now. She left her hut, walking slowly, dreading the coming meeting. In the village around her, the faces of the adults were serious, sad, worried, or angry, and even the youngest of the children were subdued. She saw Jerdon walking feebly back toward his hut, tears twisting through the wrinkled pathway of his face.

Near Emel and Marta's hut, Kara saw Lela's body on the wooden bench near the hut's door. A number of villagers were offering their condolences to Emel. Sobbing aloud, she ran toward Emel, flung herself swiftly into his arms, not to give comfort, but to find solace.

In his eyes, filled with his own grief and compassion, she found the forgiveness for her self-imposed guilt. Ashamed of her own weakness, she pulled herself away and turned to find Wer and Stephen standing behind her. She felt Wer's guilt, so similar to her own, and Stephen's rage, so powerful it tore at her mind.

"I have to go back," Stephen said, "before anyone else dies. I'll make Haley pay for this, and I will make him pay dearly." He turned to walk away, and Kara started after him. Wer caught her arm.

"Let him be, Kara. Your presence will only turn his anger into guilt he doesn't deserve."

"Wer," Kara whispered his name and looked into the soft brown eyes she had not dared to face since the mind-meld. "Forgive me."

She pulled herself out of his grip and ran toward her hut.

Feeling pain each time he even thought of Kara now, Wer turned his thoughts to his grieving friend. "Come, Emel," he said. "Let Jarta carry Lela to Jerdon so that he can prepare her for burial."

Jarta picked up the small body, and Wer took Emel by the arm and led him away. They walked aimlessly down soggy strips of land outside the village, Emel seeming to need to stay in motion, Wer's steps haunted by Kara's plea for forgiveness. The same words had been on his lips when she had spoken, and he knew each of the three of them felt the need for forgiveness for their love. He silently cursed the mind-meld that had exposed their inner thoughts.

Four hours later, the villagers gathered for Lela's funeral. Wer and Marta walked with Emel behind the bearers who carried Lela's small wrapped body slowly down the dismal path toward the dry area which was already a burial ground for two children who had died since the rebels had entered the swamp. Absorbing the pain and rage that whirled like a violent storm through his friend, Wer attempted to offer what comfort he could with the mind-touch.

Emel's words came unexpectedly into Wer's stunned mind. "I feel your pain also, Wer."

"Emel?" Wer thought the question, doubting his own mind.

"Yes. I have suspected since the mind-meld that between the five of us mental communication could go beyond images and emotions to direct speech. Marta and I have been experimenting."

Wer's thoughts immediately went to Kara. "Have you

determined if distance creates any barriers?"

"Wherever she goes," Emel, knowing exactly what Wer's real question had been, thought back to Wer, "you will be able to speak with her as if she stood beside you."

"I wonder if it is comfort or more pain you give me." Wer thought.

Emel acknowledged with a mental shrug and lost himself once more in his own pain.

Wer let his mind drift to the eerie half-lit world around him. The scents and echoing sounds of the swamp brought calm to the turmoil of his emotions. The swamp, with its teeming life, was a harsh place--not malicious--simply indifferent to man and his emotions. He reached but with his mind and drew strength from the indifference of his dark shelter.

At the soggy hole dug only an hour before, the bearers shoveled wet soil over the still, silent bundle, and Elder-Priest Mellow, avoiding Emel's eyes, spoke. "A lovely child we all cherished now lies beyond the fears and hardships we are left to face. But the soul that made her sparkle, the feelings that reached out to us are not dead; their memory remains with us. Give thanks to the gods for your time with her and for the gift of her life."

"What gods do we thank, priest?" Emel asked, turning to walk back to the village.

"Let him go," Wer thought to Marta when she moved to follow.

"Wer?"

"Who else?" he thought to her and then placed his arm tightly around her shoulder. Marta buried her face in his chest and cried for the first time since Lela's death.

Other villagers could be heard murmuring sentiments similar to Emel's. The funeral of Lela had opened up the wounds everyone suffered through the loss of their gods. Elder-Priest Mellow rapidly concluded the service, and the villagers, in bewilderment and confusion in the face of death without faith, headed home.

Wer looked over at Jerdon and saw the old man deep in concentration, muttering to himself, a slight frown on his face.

✺ · · · ✠ · · · ✻

Jerdon paced the short length of his hut while waiting for Wer to arrive. He had hoped to see the people turn away from the lies of the church, but Emel's words at Lela's burial had made him realize that, with their loss of belief in the church, the people had lost faith. Jerdon had lived long enough to learn that it was faith that most often gave people the strength to survive their hardships, and the Thetans had many hardships still to come. He had never meant for them to turn away from the gods, only the church.

In his agitation, Jerdon had left his mind unshielded, and now he felt an abrupt connection to his mental pattern, recognized the pattern of his old friend Mathis, and started to shield out of habit. Then, he sensed Mathis's fear, confusion, and desperation; he knew something was seriously wrong.

Even now, he could not desert the man who had once been his closest friend. Besides, he had a selfish motive; Mathis was the one man who could really help with the Thetans' loss of faith. Even though they had disagreed violently on church policy, Jerdon thought, Mathis had the strongest faith of any man he had ever known. Jerdon concentrated on feelings of calmness and friendship, hoping Mathis would understand more direct communication would follow.

"Jerdon," Wer said, coming through the hut door.

Jerdon kept his connection with Mathis while acknowledging Wer's presence with a nod, then said, "Things have changed since I sent for you. Stephen must leave immediately. We can't wait for morning."

"It's only a few hours until dark. Why the urgency now?" Wer asked. Jerdon could sense Wer's fear of Kara's reaction.

"I've been in contact with Mathis. I don't know what's wrong, but I know that something has happened that frightened him, and I've never known Mathis to be afraid of anything. I could pick up that Mathis felt Stephen crucial to what was happening. Kara will have to go with Stephen. Stephen will protect her to the best of his ability, and I need someone to carry a message to Mathis."

Wer looked pale and older, but his voice did not falter when he said, "We'll leave immediately."

"Take three of the horses with you. I know the dangers of riding in the swamp, particularly in the dark, but speed may be terribly important."

Jerdon stood at the door watching Wer walk away through

the darkening village. Then he turned his thoughts completely back to Mathis.

Peace is despair'd,
For who can think Submission? War then, War
Open or understood must be resolv'd.

John Milton, Paradise Lost

CHAPTER TWELVE

In the pale dawn of first suns' rise, Haley stood outside the officers' barrack just to the left of a ten-man firing-squad. Twenty feet in front of the firing-squad, six priests were tied to the twisted metal frame of the armory building the rebels had blown up on their weapons raid. Haley, in retaliation for the six men he had lost in yesterday's rescue, had decided to start the executions with six priests.

He looked at the faces of the priests before him. The youngest was the new Elder-Priest of Quaillian; his face was serene, his eyes were closed, his mouth moved, apparently in prayer. The plump, gray-haired, black priest of New Hope looked back at him with a compassionate forgiveness, and

Haley felt his anger rise. The other four, with their robes shaking from body tremors and their voices quavering as they spoke their last prayers, looked nervous enough to give Haley a feeling of triumph.

Haley turned to the tall, robed man to his left. "High-Priest," he said, making his tone of voice as mocking as possible, "if you have some last rites for the dying, I suggest you perform them now. The firing squad is ready."

Mathis, one of the few men he had known taller than himself, looked down into Haley's eyes. In Mathis's steady look, filled with sorrow, Haley saw a grim strength, void of any forgiveness. Haley knew Mathis had become a personal enemy. He would have to kill the priest soon.

Mathis finally said, "There are no rites."

Haley turned to the firing-squad. "Ready." All ten raised their ceremonial rifles into position. "Aim." Shoulders shifted slightly, eyes steadied, index fingers readied against firing mechanisms. "Fire." The sound of the weapons firing reverberated in Haley's ears while the six bodies jerked once or twice at the bullets' impact and then slumped into grotesque shapes bound by ropes to the building's frame.

He watched Mathis walk toward the bodies that now looked like hideous caricatures of the Thetan priests, dripping blood in bright red splashes on the charred pavement in front of the burned-out armory. The High-Priest's tall frame appeared slightly stooped. His long gray hair, sparkling silver in the shafts of suns-rise, looked grayer and wilder than before. Mathis looked almost as changed now from the way he had looked a few minutes ago as the six hanging before him.

"Mathis," Haley said, and the priest turned. Two lines that Haley had not noticed before were etched in Mathis's face, one running from each cheek bone to jaw. "Take the bodies back to their villages for burial. I want the villagers to see them."

Mathis began untying the ropes around the body of Blade, the young Quaillian priest.

The cavalcade of ground transport vehicles moved rapidly across the New Mexico desert toward the military spaceport. In the back seat of his personal vehicle, placed in the center of the line of armed military vehicles, Jason McNamara looked out at the desert which had only in the last ten years started to show signs of ecological stability. He was grateful that he, unlike the McNamaras before him, had lived to see evidence of Earth's recovery. Now, he only hoped that the McNamara line would be around when recovery was complete. Jackson, carefully checking the packets of written orders to be given to Bishop Harrold and Commander Yen Sing, sat beside him.

When the cavalcade swung through the curved drive leading to the spaceport gate, Jackson spoke. "Sir, the orders make no mention of Stephen. If he is there when the ship arrives, are you planning to have him return home?"

"I can't make that decision yet, Jackson. If the boy returns, he'll contact me. Then I'll decide."

"Are there any personal messages you would like to send?"

"No, just meet me after you're finished."

Jackson said no more; the cavalcade had come to a stop. Soldiers got out of the other vehicles and went into formation around the Premier's ground transport. A soldier opened the door for McNamara. McNamara doubled his tall frame to get out and then stood waiting for Jackson.

"I'll meet you on the observation deck as soon as I've delivered the orders, sir," Jackson said.

In front of the spaceport observation building, fifteen minutes later, McNamara and Jackson watched the giant transport ship lift silently and majestically into the cloudless sky and dwindle to a tiny speck.

Back at the Government House in Communications Central, McNamara sat in the transmission-screen chair and said to Jackson, "I want recordings in triplicate of every transmission to or from Theta until this situation is settled."

"Yes, sir," Jackson replied. He moved to the Chief Technician's side and gave the order for visual link with the Thetan base.

In minutes, the face of the Thetan Communication Officer appeared on the screen before the Premier. The face moved. "Thetan Base responding," said the voice coming from speakers behind McNamara's head.

"Has your Commander returned?" McNamara asked.

"No, sir," said the voice from the speakers.

"Put Colonel Haley on screen," he said, knowing his voice sounded old and tired.

McNamara watched the screen as Haley's face replaced the face of the Communication Technician's.

"Colonel," McNamara said as soon as the change was completed, "a ship has just departed for Theta; ETA is three-hundred sixty hours. Commander Yen-Sing is aboard with two hundred of his best soldiers and will take command if Commander McNamara has not returned. Bishop Harrold is also on board and will begin integrating the Thetan church into the True Church. Have all the officials of the Thetan church available to him on his arrival."

"Yes, sir," Haley replied. McNamara noticed the strained sound of Haley's voice and the sparkling signs of perspiration visible on the forehead of his transmission screen image.

"Have you any news about my grandson?" he asked.

"No, sir," Haley said, "but I am currently, ah, negotiating with the locals and expect to have secured his release before the ship arrives."

McNamara had not missed Haley's hesitation before he said "negotiating," and he had not missed the twitch in Haley's hard jaw muscles. He knew Haley thought only in military terms and knew that Haley's type of "negotiation" would probably involve force. Force was acceptable to McNamara as long as it didn't endanger Stephen's life, if he was still alive. "Good luck," he said. "I expect to be informed immediately of any news concerning my grandson."

McNamara signaled for the technician to end the transmission and rose from the chair. Jackson followed him as he left the room. In the elevator, McNamara pushed the fiftieth-floor button, and the elevator started its climb to his office.

"Sir," Jackson said, "you've been working almost round-the-clock for days now. Shouldn't you rest?"

"You know as well as I do that we've let other things go for the past week while we worked on the Thetan situation. We have eight planets besides Theta, and they all have problems. I'll rest when we've caught up." Then, more to himself than to Jackson, he added, "Besides, preoccupation with work takes your mind away from your personal worries."

Three hours after full suns-rise, Stephen guided his horse to the rise of dry ground just outside the edge of the swamp east of the base. Ahead of him, Kara and Wer reined their horses to a stop.

"I'll leave you here," Wer said.

Stephen watched Kara, her eyes looking toward the plateau's top a mile away. He knew all three of them were consciously avoiding each other's eyes. He looked at Wer and said, "Take care, Wer."

He felt Wer's knowledge of all the love and shame that the words failed to express.

"Take care yourself." Wer's words came directly into his mind. His mind unable to accept that Wer was speaking directly into his mind, Stephen simply stood looking at Wer.

"I should have mind-spoken to you or Kara sooner," came Wer's next words, "but what is between us made contact difficult."

Stephen could feel Wer's difficulty, the emotions that made the mind-speech so painful. Stephen's pain was almost identical.

"I'm sorry," Stephen thought to Wer.

"It's all right, Stephen. None of us can prevent what we feel. No one's to blame." Wer smiled at Stephen, leaned over and placed his hand on Stephen's shoulder, then curbed his horse and left.

"Kara," Stephen said not yet ready to attempt mind-speech with her, "Let's go."

He could sense how much Kara needed to share with him, but he could also sense that she was not emotionally ready for such a sharing. He merely said aloud, "Everything's going to be all right. You'll see."

"I know," she said, but he sensed her doubt as he knew she sensed his. He knew his grandfather too well to believe that the Premier would change policy because his grandson thought such a change was needed.

They rode in silence the rest of the way to the base, urging Shade and Stephen's tired horse to the fastest pace possible up the side of the plateau. Under the breezy shade of the trees his breath came easier than it had during the past few days in the muggy swamp, but his thoughts came no easier.

He shied away from thoughts of his grandfather; his fear of

Jason McNamara was a lifelong habit that he could not easily overcome. Haley was a different matter. He intended to see Haley court-martialed for causing the death of Emel's young sister. He also intended to change conditions for the Thetans before any more lives were lost. Of course, any changes in policy on Theta would have to go through his grandfather, and challenging the old man was something he couldn't even envision yet.

Not for the first time, thoughts of his grandfather led him to wonder what the old man's reaction to Kara would be. But even if it meant he had to forsake his other plans and flee with her back to the swamp, he intended to marry her.

On the outskirts of the base, Stephen could see a crowd, military personnel and locals, around what had been the armory building. Then he saw a thin, young woman tied to one of the building's remaining frame supports and a firing squad, guns ready to fire, which faced her.

He kicked his horse for greater speed and shouted with the full force of his lungs. But the guns fired, and horrified, he watched the woman's body twitch and slide down against the ropes. His horse carried him through the crowd to Haley's side, and he reined in, slung his right leg over the horse's neck, and slid to the ground.

Clenching his fists, he faced Haley and watched conflicting emotions from satisfaction to irritation flicker briefly in the eyes of Haley's immobile face. In his outrage, Stephen could find no words.

"Commander," Haley said, "The Premier will be pleased to see our efforts have resulted in your release."

Stephen had meant to have Haley put under arrest immediately, but if Haley had been acting on the Premier's orders, he could not be arrested. Controlling his frustration and rage, Stephen turned to the firing squad and said, "Release any Thetans that you are holding."

Then he turned back to Haley and said, "Colonel, you will accompany me to the communication building for a transmission to the Premier."

For the first time, he attempted mind-speech with Kara. "Kara," he thought.

"Stephen?" came the bewildered question of Kara's first mind-speech.

"Yes. I'll explain later. For now just stay close to me," Stephen thought back to her while he walked toward the communication building.

Haley made an attempt to block Kara's entrance into the communication building, and Stephen turned back and, looking directly into Haley's eyes, said, "You will never interfere with this woman in any way."

Then he reached around Haley and pulled Kara to his side before turning back to the communication technician.

"Establish contact with Communication Central," he said, sitting in the transmission-screen chair.

Stephen watched the face from home appear on the screen and say, "Communication Central responding."

"This is Planetary Commander McNamara," Stephen said, making the unnecessary customary identification. "Please inform the Premier of my transmission and request that he make a return transmission."

"The Premier will arrive momentarily, sir. Please stand by."

Stephen watched the face disappear from the screen and looked over at Kara, giving a mental reassurance. When he looked back at the screen, his grandfather's face was already visible.

"Commander," his grandfather said, showing no emotion, "I'm glad to see you've made a safe return," and Stephen felt the familiar disappointment at his grandfather's greeting which indicated no more concern than the Premier would express for any other of his military personnel. "Now, what about the rebel situation on Theta?"

"The rebels have ceased all hostilities, sir," Stephen answered. "I have given my word on new negotiations for their services in grain production and promised the rebels full immunity for any acts committed in the rebellion."

"Such generous promises will undermine your authority, Commander," McNamara said, "but we'll discuss the situation further, after I've had time to assess the situation."

"Sir," Stephen said, "I am having Colonel Haley arrested for the execution of Thetan citizens in my absence."

"No, Commander, you will not," McNamara said. "Colonel Haley was acting Commander in your absence, and his actions, I believe, resulted in your return."

"Then, sir," Stephen said. "May I request that Colonel Haley be transferred off Theta?"

"Put the request in writing and send it through the proper channels. You will be notified of the decision."

"Sir, I also have a personal request. I would like to submit my permission request for marriage," Stephen said and watched his grandfather's face closely for any indication of how the request was received. Even though it lasted for only a fraction of a second, Stephen caught the narrowing of his grandfather's eyes.

"The request is for marriage to a local girl, one of the rebels?" his grandfather asked.

"Yes, sir."

"Did you make this arrangement as part of your release from the rebels?"

"No, sir. I'm in love with her."

His grandfather hesitated only briefly before he said, "Bishop Harrold will be arriving in two weeks. After he has talked with the girl, we'll discuss the matter again."

"Grandfather," Stephen said quietly, using the form of address he had not used since he was five, "I am marrying Kara immediately, with or without Federation permission."

"Surely, you can wait a couple of weeks, since you obviously haven't known the girl but days," his grandfather said with irritation rising in his voice.

Stephen knew he had to marry Kara immediately to protect her with the rebellion still unsettled, and he knew in two weeks time his grandfather might do anything. "I plan to marry Kara tomorrow. If it means I resign my position and move to the swamp, that's what I'll do."

Feeling in some ways like he was five again, he waited for his grandfather's reply.

Jason McNamara looked at the defiance in his grandson's eyes, at the stubborn set of his jaw. He almost couldn't hide his elation; he had almost given up hope of ever seeing the boy show enough courage to challenge him on anything. He asked, "Is the girl there with you?"

"Yes, sir," Stephen answered, "and her name is Kara."

"Put her in the chair. I want to talk to her."

The Premier studied the face that appeared on the screen. She was a pretty girl, and young, much younger than he had expected, but there was nothing soft or weak in her youthful face. Her eyes showed no fear as she looked back at his image on the transmission screen. McNamara thought he knew where his grandson's new-found courage had come from. He wasn't going to let this girl get away from Stephen.

"Kara," he said, "are you willing to come to Earth and learn the duties of the First Lady?"

"I am willing to be Stephen's wife," the girl answered, "and I will go wherever he has to go."

She was playing word games with him, McNamara thought, a good sign that she wasn't in the least bit intimidated by the Premier of the Federation. The girl had the kind of strength he had hoped to see brought into the family before his son had married. This girl would give him strong great-grandchildren, and he could justify the marriage as a political move for a stronger alliance with Theta.

"Thank you for speaking with me, Kara," he said to the girl's image. "Would you have my grandson return to the chair, please."

When Stephen's image returned to the screen, McNamara said, "Permission granted, but the service must be conducted by your True Church Officer and broadcast over a live transmission. The marriage of the next Premier is a public event. This evening's news program will carry the announcement. You will hold the service in twenty-four hours."

After he ended the transmission, Jason McNamara allowed himself a private, satisfied smile.

For never can true reconcilement grow
Where wounds of deadly hate have pierc'd so deep:

John Milton, *Paradise Lost*

CHAPTER THIRTEEN

Yesterday, after he had delivered the bodies of the six priests, Mathis had returned to the base to find that another hostage had been executed and that Stephen McNamara had returned. About an hour later, Kara had delivered Jerdon's message, and told him Wer wanted to talk with him and would meet him at the edge of the swamp near sunsdown today.

This morning he had gone to visit Stephen in his office for a private talk. Listening to Stephen's promises and his optimistic outlook for Theta's future, Mathis had felt sorry for the young Planetary Commander who had no concept of how serious the problems on Theta were. New negotiations for labor and grain production would be small help to a culture already destroyed by internal problems, if the new negotiations could even be worked out.

Stephen obviously had little understanding of his grandfather, but Mathis had no problem understanding the Premier. On a smaller scale, Mathis's own position had been equivalent to Jason McNamara's, and the former High-Priest knew that the Premier would not let any feelings he might have for his grandson interfere with decisions concerning the Federation any more than he, as High-Priest, had allowed his nephew's pleas and, finally, banishment, to interfere with decisions concerning Theta and the Church.

He had left Stephen's office both saddened and inspired by the young man's hope and gone to talk with Kara before he left to meet Wer at the edge of the swamp.

Mathis watched Kara stare out of the small window of the gray-walled quarters in the officer's barrack where she had spent the previous night.

"I wish I could remain for your wedding," he said. "But Wer will be waiting for me by the time I make it to the swamp's edge."

"I have no need of a priest," Kara said.

"I meant as a friend, Kara," he said. "But I hope you understand it was the humans, and not the gods, who failed you."

Without taking her eyes off the window, she asked, "Are the gods real?"

"I'm not sure anymore, Kara," he said, feeling the truth

of his answer. "The only thing I'm still sure of is that some things are worth holding on to."

She made no answer, so he quietly left her quarters.

Within half-an-hour, he was riding down the side of the plateau anxious to see Wer again. Close to the edge of the swamp, he spotted Wer, sitting with his back against a tree trunk.

Mathis dismounted, and Wer stood up and took a step to his side.

"Hello, Uncle," Wer said.

"Hello, Wer," Mathis said, reaching for his nephew both physically and mentally. His hands rested easily on Wer's shoulders, but his mind-touch met only Wer's shield. "It's good to see you." He looked around. "Don't you have a horse?"

"No," Wer answered, "and you need to go with me into the swamp to talk with Jerdon. You'll have to lead your roan and hold on tightly; most of the horses were uncontrollable their first few days in the swamp."

While they walked, Mathis listened to Wer tell about how the people in the swamp villages had adapted and utilized the resources of the swamp. The boy had been right about the potential of the swamp.

Mathis looked closely at the swamp around him, a place forbidden to him all his life. Wer lead him through the swamp on a winding path of ground through the stagnant water; gray stumps and large vines were heavy across the water and most of the ground that rose occasionally from the water. Ample evidence of animal life was everywhere; animals that Wer assured him offered food sources for the rebels. What bothered him were the tall gray trees that made a dark canopy between him and the sky where he had always believed the gods lived.

"But," he heard Wer saying, "Stephen has promised that there will be no reprisals for their rebellion and that there will be new work conditions for grain production, and now most of the people are planning to return home."

"No," Mathis said more sharply than he intended. His mind was reeling so much from his fear of the rebels returning that he could barely find the words to express himself to Wer. "Stephen doesn't have a large enough force right now to protect any returning rebels."

Wer stopped and turned around to face him. "What do you mean? Protect them from what?"

"Six priests and a young mother of three have been executed and Lela killed because of your actions, Wer," Mathis answered slowly, trying hard to find the words that would make Wer see the truth of the situation in the villages. "The people are divided now between those who blame the rebels for the deaths and those who blame the Earthmen. The church officials, especially the new High-Priest, and most of the Twelve Disciples, fear the return of the rebels. They have been able to convince most of those still in the villages that you and Jerdon have tricked the rebels into believing lies about the Holy Books."

"But," Mathis continued, "if the rebels return in great

number, the church will be threatened, and I can't decide how the new High-Priest will react. Hsit is a dangerous man. And Stephen, at least for the next two weeks, faces problems of his own, especially with the man who is his second in command and the soldiers who lost friends in your rebellion."

Wer looked at him for a moment. "I suppose hoping everything would suddenly return to normal was unrealistic," he said and grinned wistfully.

Then Mathis saw his nephew go rigid.

"Wer?" he asked, wondering if they were in danger. "Wer, what's wrong?"

Wer's body relaxed. "Kara's wedding is about to begin."

Mathis remembered how he had thought at one time that Wer and Kara might marry. He was sorry for his nephew, but he was wondering how Wer could have known the precise moment Kara's wedding would start. They started moving again down the swamp trail.

Kara stood just inside the Communications Building and remembered the young red-haired Seraph that she and Shade had killed here and how much her life and her world had changed since that day. In a few minutes, she would marry in this building, in many ways forsaking the war she had begun for love of the enemy.

She felt strange in the odd white dress and sheer cloth on

her head covering her face, both made by a young group of Seraphs, or soldiers she supposed she must learn to call them, under Stephen's command. They had been surprisingly endearing in their eagerness to see that she was properly dressed for a wedding to their commander that would be transmitted to eight other worlds scattered through a space she could still not comprehend even with Stephen's memories. Working through the night, they had used linens and sheer curtains from the officers' dining quarters as well as personal items to come up with garments that they thought would do them and their commander proud when seen on the other worlds.

When Stephen walked in, he didn't mind-speak, but as he walked around inspecting the room other young soldiers had decorated for the ceremony, she felt his love surround her and his excitement about their wedding and the future he envisioned for them. The wall across from the communication equipment had been covered with cloth; an array of greenery from around the area covered the cloth, and in front of the wall was a platform the length of the wall about four feet wide. In the center of the platform was an archway made from two trees about twelve feet tall secured to the platform about five feet apart with their tops bent over each other and tied together to make an arch a little more than six foot high in the center. Vines and flowers were intertwined over the entire arch. Kara didn't know what the people from other worlds would think of it, but she thought it was the most beautiful thing she had ever seen.

"Kara," Stephen mind-spoke to her, "come stand beside me under the arch."

Stephen reached out for her hand as soon as she was near

enough, and his touch erased all her nervousness. They stood under the arch, side-by-side, hand-in-hand, while the True Church Officer positioned himself in front of them but below the platform so the camera would transmit his head with Stephen's face and hers just above his head, looking toward the camera.

As soon as the Communications Officer had a transmission line open to Earth, a screen was turned on that covered the wall above the Communications equipment, displaying the current broadcast from Earth being sent to all planets in the Federation. A man was on the screen, standing outside a huge ornate building, seeming to be looking out at them. He was talking about the Premier and his guests inside the building waiting for the marriage of the Premier's grandson coming to them live from the planet of Theta.

"The Premier's diplomats on Theta," the man was saying, "have worked diligently to finalize a contract for Stephen McNamara's wedding to the daughter of a high ranking official of Theta which will ensure closer relationships between the newly re-found colony and the other Federation planets. The rumor about the contract is that it will guarantee increasing amounts of raw food supplies will be shipped from our most fertile plant, easing food shortages for the rest of us."

"I've just received information that the wedding is about to begin, so we'll be switching over to the inside of the church, where the Premier and his guest are participating in the wedding."

Kara almost choked keeping back the laughter over the elaborate lies concerning her marriage, as the face she had seen for the first time yesterday filled the screen. She understood where the Thetan priest's ability to fool their people came from. She supposed deception might be a trait of all humans.

The screen split in two, and she saw her face, Stephen's, and the Church Officer's appear opposite the Premier. The Officer raised a bell and rang it three times; then asked, "Who gives permission for this marriage?"

Kara watched Stephen's grandfather stand and say, "I, Jason McNamara, Premier of the Federation, give permission for this marriage." She felt Stephen's surprise and mentally linked with him.

"He looks pleased." Stephen thought to her. "I don't know why, and that worries me."

"It feels more like panic." Kara returned. "You think he's planning on using our marriage for something bad."

Kara stayed linked to Stephen, each feeling their love, only dimly aware of the Officer reading the wedding rite. Then, Stephen squeezed her hand and thought, "Say I do."

Finally, Stephen drew her close to him and bent down and put his lips on hers. Their minds were totally shielded, and they were aware of nothing except the oneness of their souls and the physical sensations of their bodies pressed together.

∽ · · · �֎ · · · ⊱

Mathis led his horse slowly behind Wer's horse down the damp trail that made him jerk at every sound and flicker of movement. His nephew seemed reluctant to talk except for occasional instructions on navigating the swamp. So, Mathis walked lost in his own thoughts

He knew the reason the church had forbidden entry into the swamp, but that reason was, perhaps, long since gone. In the early days, the number of Thetans had been so small that every death had been a blow to their chances of survival. The original settlers had come from a planet based on technology where true wilderness no longer existed. They had not had the skills to survive a wilderness as harsh as the swamp.

He could see the beauty of the swamp that Wer had always seen, but he was nervous, knowing the dangers, especially for someone like him. He had been taken to New Hope as a small boy to be educated and trained as a scientist in either the parapsychology or computer labs, so he had less outdoors skills than most Thetans.

He thought about his training as a boy. The six ships that had come to Theta from Earth had carried not only the settlers which had been identified as having psychic abilities, but also enough specialist and supplies to begin constructing a city with the highest technology available. Later supply ships had been scheduled to bring the supplies for further construction, but had never come. In each generation after, a number of young Thetans had been selected to be trained to replace the scientist and technicians. He had been one and had seen the components stripped from the old ships to keep the original equipment running. He had been in his teens and in training as a computer specialist.

But his interest had been the gods. He had been twenty when he had been allowed to join the priesthood. His entire life since that day had been the survival of his people and his personal quest to find the truth of the gods. Now, walking through the swamp, he could only see those long years in terms of failure.

"We're at the closest village." Wer's voice broke into his thoughts.

"Good," he replied. "I'm an old man for an eight hour walk."

Then, he stepped into an area only slightly cleared with about twenty scattered huts and two large fire pits. He looked around at the people and saw his old friend, Jerdon, sitting outside a hut talking with two children.

Wer was walking straight toward Jerdon, and Mathis continued to walk behind. He watched Jerdon slowly rise, but he moved better than Mathis had seen him move in almost two decades.

"Wer, you've traveled fast," Jerdon said. Then he looked at Mathis, took three steps to reach him, placed his hands on Mathis's arms, and said, "Mathis, my friend."

Mathis felt the muscles of his heart contract and realized that until that moment he had not known how deeply the rift in their friendship had hurt him.

"Jerdon," he said. "What a fool I have been."

"Not a fool, Mathis, a seeker," Jerdon said. "Come into my home and have something to eat."

Jerdon turned to Wer, "Wer, let your uncle rest a bit and then come back with Marta and Emel, and let's hear Mathis's news."

Mathis watched Wer turn and walk away, leading both of their horses. He turned to Jerdon and said, "I think Wer may never forgive me for the damage I've done him."

"Wer's the finest and strongest person I've ever known," Jerdon said. "Twenty years ago, I said that same thing about you. The two of you will work things out. Now, come in and have something to eat."

After he had eaten, Mathis felt awkward alone with Jerdon. He wanted to say something to more than apologize for the things he had said when Jerdon left the priesthood and for his coldness since. But, Jerdon was talking easily about the rapid construction of the villages in the swamp, about how Wer had known how to locate the villages so that they were not visible from above, and how the people had adapted to life in the swamp.

"Jerdon," he heard Wer's voice outside Jerdon's door.

"Come in, Wer," Jerdon called.

Mathis watched his nephew come through the door followed by Emel and Marta. He was startled by Marta's appearance. He lurched toward her but stopped himself.

"Marta," he said, reaching out to her. "Are you well?"

The question sounded trite to his ears, but that was the best he could think to ask. He had been horrified by Marta's rape and devastated by her growing insanity. That incident had triggered his first meeting with the council to propose the idea that the people should be told the truth about the men they called Seraphs and his most serious argument with the former military commander from Earth. He had wanted the men punished by Thetan law, but that had not happened.

"Yes, High Priest Mathis," Marta replied with no kindness in her voice. "I am well. But, perhaps, had you told us the truth in the beginning, I would never have been harmed."

He felt his own guilt for her suffering, but could think of no words to offer her when he heard Jerdon speak.

"Marta, I also knew the truth, as did Wer. It was not Mathis, but the council, that started and continued the lies. All three of us, however, are guilty of obeying the order to keep our knowledge secret. Now, we are all sorry for that mistake."

Mathis looked into Emel's eyes and saw rage and pain directed at him. "Emel," he said, "I will never ask that you forgive me, but I will ask that you tolerate me and accept what help I can offer in this dangerous situation we all face."

He watched Emel's eyes soften from rage to kindness while the pain there remained.

Wer, who had remained silent since entering the hut, said, "Well, Uncle, I believe we all accept we have a common cause, so why don't we all sit down and hear what you have to say."

Mathis smiled slightly at Wer, grateful that he had ended the painful greeting, and was the first to sit. He waited until everyone else was sitting before he spoke.

"First, you three younger people must understand exactly the way the council works and the dangers of Hsit becoming High Priest. I need to tell you about my personal knowledge of Haley and why I think he is a direct threat, not only to the rebels and villagers, but, more immediately, to Stephen and, by association, Kara."

He explained the way the church and the researchers were a unified group within the council, how the council was made up of members drawn from each group, and how they were selected. He told them of Hsit's plan to negotiate with the research information and promises of increased grain production to gain more authority for himself over the people of Theta and his plan to basically enslave his own people to get control of the grain production. He tried to describe Haley as accurately as possible and to what lengths a man so cruel and ambitious might go to remove any threat to him that he perceived. He explained how Stephen had become Haley's greatest threat the minute he returned from the rebel camp alive and in sympathy with the rebels.

Finally, he said, "I learned a great deal about the Premier from the last military commander here. I think I understand him. His position and responsibilities are very similar to mine when I was the High Priest, though on a much larger scale. My opinion of the man, based on his decisions I've been aware of, is that he is a fair and just man whose primary objective is the continued survival of more than thirty billion humans scattered over a number of damaged planets. I don't believe personal sentiments, such as the welfare or desires of a grandson, would ever deter him from making decisions he feels are best for the whole of humanity. The grain from Theta is now critical to the survival of millions."

"In light of my belief about the Premier," he continued, "my opinion is that we adhere strictly to a truce and keep abreast of everything happening outside the swamp. I have a group of priest loyal to me and sympathetic to the rebellion that I can contact to keep us informed on what Hsit and the council are doing and planning and on what's going on in the villages and fields. Where I fear we'll have problems is communication with Stephen and Kara and knowing what Haley might be planning."

Wer spoke, "Don't worry about that. Emel, Marta, and I already have a system in place for communication with Stephen and Kara. They are not alone there."

"What is your system," Mathis asked.

"Sorry, Uncle, the three of us, well, we feel that we should keep our system secret for a little while."

Mathis was not surprised that Wer would not confide in him, but he saw the surprised look on Jerdon's face and knew that Wer and the others were also keeping secrets from Jerdon.

So frown'd the mighty Combatants, that Hell
Grew darker at their frown, so matcht they stood;

John Milton, Paradise Lost

CHAPTER FOURTEEN

Hsit sat in the High Priest chair at the long table in Visionsite's great meeting room alone and in utter frustration. His plan had been to approach young McNamara when he was rescued from the rebels, or the next commander if he was dead, with a proposal that he be the Governor of Theta, as well as, Head of the True Church on Theta, in exchange for guaranteed grain shipment and information about Theta's research program and continued work in that area. Now, Hsit thought, that idiot young Commander had returned besotted with a girl from the rebel group. He had known as soon as they had announced the two would marry the very next day that he was running out of time to negotiate with the Federation.

In desperation he had sent a message to Haley requesting a secret meeting and suggesting he could help him with his problems. He had not decided exactly what he would propose to Haley or how much he would reveal of his own plans. He didn't totally trust Haley.

Now, only one day after the wedding, the first sun rose with him still sitting in the council meeting room, still undecided on what he would say to Haley. He rose from the table and walked to the stables to have his horse readied for a ride.

Just as the second sun was just above the tree tops, Hsit drew near the bottom of the plateau and saw Haley waiting out in the open. He rode on until he was near enough for Haley to hear his speaking voice.

"Haley, thank you for meeting me," he said. "But, I suggest we move into that grove of evergreens to your left. It could be awkward for both of us if we were seen in a private meeting."

When they were a short distanced into the cover of the grove, Hsit stopped his horse and dismounted, and Haley followed his lead.

"Now, High Priest," Haley said, "Your message implied you had some information for me that would help solve the rebel problem."

"Yes," Hsit said. "Since I am now the High Priest, I can bring the rebels in and punish through the church. That will convince the rest of our people that the punishment is from the gods, and they will be content to work in the fields, so we can promise increased grain shipments. In exchange, I would want to negotiate a new arrangement with the Federation. The church does have an even greater bargaining point that you would be the first to know about, for which we would want a little more control of our own planet, including who was Military Commander here. We would, of course, suggest you."

"Haley," he continued, "I think this will put both of us in a position of more power. If you are the one who implements a new treaty, you should receive some type of promotion; I believe you and I could deal well together."

Haley looked at him closely before speaking, "Several recent developments stand in the way of your plan, High Priest."

Hsit felt a sense of dread tighten his throat.

"First," Haley continued, "if the truce between Commander McNamara and the rebels holds and if the rebels return to their villages, the power of your church will be weakened. Also, the Premier is sending troops along with Federation Commander Yin-Sing, a ruthless man, totally dedicated to the Premier. Since that ship also brings Bishop Harrold and a hundred priest for the purpose of establishing the True Church here on Theta, I believe the Federation Commander plans to simply destroy your church."

Hsit felt his entire body quiver in panic at Haley's words. But, he kept his voice calm and asked, "And what will this Yin-Sing's takeover of the planet do to your career, Colonel.

Haley again studied his face before answering, "It won't be the best scenario for me. So, I do think we could aid each other. Our biggest problem, as I see it, is the truce holding until Federation Commander Yin-Sing arrives. However, if the hostilities have resumed, the Federation Commander will discount most of what young McNamara has to say and, I think, consult me on what has been happening on Theta and ask for my input on what I think would be the best solution."

"The rebels won't break the truce," Hsit interrupted, "not with Kara inside your base and the former High Priest in the swamp."

"But," Haley said, "one rebel looks like any other rebel. Some of your villagers, some totally dedicated to your gods, might be able to be convinced that they could serve their gods by making their own attacks on our personnel. Such action would destroy the truce."

Hsit thought furiously before answering. Haley's proposal offered far more danger than he had planned on placing himself, but if something didn't happen fast, he stood to lose everything.

"I will need some time to think about this and see how a few of the more fanatical believers react to some subtle suggestions. I think we should meet again."

"We'll meet here then," Haley said, "in one week."

Hsit watched Haley mount his horse and ride away before leaving the grove in a different direction. He was still shaken by the new knowledge that the destruction of the church now sped through space towards him. At least Haley offered some hope that he could prevent that and still attain his goal of increased power.

He could think immediately of about twenty fanatics he would recruit who could be convinced that their attacks on the Seraphs would end the rebellion and bring their fellow Thetans back to the gods.

Stephen watched Kara standing in a shaft of sunlight coming through the bedroom window while she dressed in some of the clothes they had found for her in the storeroom. It didn't matter, he thought, that the clothes were too large; she was still the most beautiful thing he had ever seen.

They had been married for ten days, but some moments he felt like she had always been there, and other times he felt he had just found her in that moment.

"I can sense you standing there thinking about me and watching," she said aloud.

"Can you see how beautiful you are through my eyes?" he thought back.

"I can see how beautiful you think I am, you silly Seraph, and you can see the way I see and love you."

He laughed out loud.

"Kara," he said. "Even with all our troubles here, I'm sure I am the happiest man who ever lived. I think we should take these clothes back off and spend the rest of the morning making love with our minds linked."

He mentally reached out and felt the desire in her stir while she thought of the intensity of their love making while their minds were linked, each able to feel the sensations and desires of the other. Then, he heard her thoughts turn to the seriousness of their situation on Theta and what it might mean for them. He felt her break the link between them.

"Stephen," she spoke aloud. "What do you think is going to happen?"

"I think I'm going to forget about sex for the rest of the day and go to my office and finish the report I'm writing for the Premier, and…."

"Your grandfather," Kara interrupted.

"No, Kara," he said. "The man who will read and judge this report is the Premier. The fact he received it from his biological grandson will not sway his decisions one way or the other. But, I'm being as persuasive as I know how to be in this report and plan on being able to send it before the day is over."

Kara walked over and put her arms around him, and he hugged her fiercely back, flooding her mind with his love.

"I love you," she said.

"And, I think," he said, "that I've loved you since the first second I saw you on the viewing screen, racing across Olhair's Valley after you destroyed our communication equipment. Thank God Wer was there to get you to safety in the swamp."

He felt her stiffen and totally shield her mind before she pulled away and turned to look out the window.

"We've never talked about Wer," he said, "but I think we should. Wer's the only real friend I've ever had and your life-long friend."

Kara turned back to him with tears rolling down her face and said, "I feel so horrible and guilty and sad everytime I even think of Wer. He's been not only my friend, but my best friend, for my entire life. Now, I can't even look into his eyes."

"He is our friend, Kara, I mind speak with him every day. Wer is a good man, and I know we cause him pain, but he doesn't blame either of us for what happened. He'll get over the pain, and the woman who loves him will show up one day."

"I hope you're right," Kara said.

"I'm always right," he teased. "Now, I've got to make myself go to work. What are you planning to do today?"

She laughed, "Private Pierson, who I think likes me a little, is coming to show me how to use the stuff in this 'kitchen' room and how to cook some things out of the food supplies from Earth. I was going to surprise you with a delicious and very private meal tonight. But, don't really expect the delicious part."

He laughed and kissed her before going to the door. At the door, he turned back and said, "Don't worry too much about the food. It's the very private part I'll be looking forward to all day."

He walked across the base to his office without really seeing anything he passed. He was mentally consumed with, not only his love for Kara, but also with his worry about the other Thetans he was bound to in friendship and love through the telepathic link they shared. They had all agreed to keep their link secret until they understood it better and knew its limits. So, he couldn't include that in the report he was sending, but he was going to include the research that the "Church" had been conducting for more than three hundred years.

He hoped that such significant new information, along with his evidence taken from Federation records here of mishandling of the original negotiations and later abuses of the Thetan people during the occupation, would be enough to at least cause the Premier to consent to a video conference with him and Mathis. Mathis had been the High Priest and had not been a part of the rebellion. His entry into the swamp had marked the beginning of the truce.

He feared, though, that even in such a scenario, the Federation would insist on punishment for some of the leaders of the revolution. His grandfather would protect Kara, he was sure, but he feared for Wer and Emel. If that threat ever became imminent, he would tell his grandfather everything about their telepathic link. It wouldn't matter to him what use the knowledge be applied; it only mattered that his friends live.

Yin-Sing walked down the main corridor of the ship to his small office. He was apprehensive about this mission, not only was it critical to the man he served and admired, it was personal. Yin-Sing had watched Stephen grow up as part of his duties. His family, since the Global Wars, had served the McNamara family as heads of the military. He had always seen his loyalty as to the McNamara family, not the Federation.

Yin-Sing knew he had never actually loved anyone, not even his wife, until he watched young Stephen growing into the man he would become. The boy had a kindness and goodness in him, usually found only in the very innocent, that he never lost even in the face of his harsh training and loneliness. He knew the Premier feared Stephen was too weak to hold the Federation together after he was gone, but Yin-Sing had seen Stephen's strength in his ability to stand true to who he was through his grandfather's disapproval of many of the boy's decisions. Yin-Sing did not want this mission to turn into a conflict between him and Stephen, his future Premier and the only person he loved.

"Federation Commander."

He looked up to see Lt. Gordon, his assistant for the past ten years, standing in his doorway.

"Come in, Gordon, and close the door."

Yin-Sing had asked Gordon to meet with him today. They would arrive on Theta in five days, and he didn't want any mistakes. He wasn't worried about his eight Commanders or the eight twenty-four man Special Forces units under their command. But, Bishop Harrold and his hundred priests was a different matter.

"Sit down, Gordon," he said. "We don't need rigid protocol behind closed doors."

He watched his assistant lower his tall, dark body into the other chair. He trusted Gordon implicitly, yet he knew little about him. Gordon spoke little, and never about his private life, but when he did speak, his words were to the point and clear.

"I want you to go over the orders for our initial few days on

Theta with the Commanders," Yin-Sing said, "then, observe them drilling those orders to their units. I want as little interaction as possible between the Special Forces and the soldiers under Commander McNamara, and absolutely no conflict."

"I'll be spending the next few days with Bishop Harrold and his priest," he continued. "Our good Bishop, as always, has arrogantly assumed he is in charge of this mission. I intend on correcting his misassumption for him and for his priests."

"Yes, sir," Gordon said and rose to leave.

"One more thing," Yin-Sing spoke quietly. "While I don't want our troops interacting with the planetary troops, I want you staying with the planetary officers as much as possible. Keep your eyes and ears open and let me know if there might be an enemy to the next Premier among his officers."

Gordon left and Yin-Sing leaned back in his chair, suddenly cold inside.

Haley glanced back once more. He was sure no one had seen him leave the base, but he wanted no witnesses to connect him to Hsit. The new High-Priest had first contacted him about a week ago, a week after Stephen McNamara had married the local savage, to discuss their mutual problem of McNamara's return. Haley had discovered Hsit could be very useful, and hoped the outcome of the coming meeting would eliminate the threat of court martial he still faced over his actions during Stephen's absence. He knew the Premier would only stay neutral in the disagreement between Stephen and himself until Commander Yen-Sing investigated and assessed the decision for the executions.

He was almost to the meeting place when he spotted Hsit in a thick grove of evergreens at the base of the plateau.

"Colonel," Hsit spoke when Haley drew near, "I'm glad you could meet me here. It could be awkward for both of us if anyone overheard our discussion."

"Have you considered what the return of the rebels will do to your authority, Hsit?" Haley asked.

"I think we can help each other," Hsit said, and Haley waited for him to continue, knowing already that the suggestions he had planted at their first meeting had taken root. The conversation went as Haley had hoped. Hsit had followers who would instigate new hostilities which could be blamed on the rebels; Stephen's truce with the rebels would appear to be broken and Yen-Sing would not question Haley's executions of the woman and six priests. "After our plans have succeeded," Hsit said, "I will give you the information I spoke of earlier, the truth which the church has kept secret for three hundred years."

At parting, Haley promised Hsit's safety and authority over all aspects of governing Theta as long as grain production met expected quotas. Haley knew he had no way of keeping such a commitment. But he knew too that Hsit was a loose end that he would have to take care of eventually.

The priest then left, and Haley watched him moving rapidly toward Olhair's Valley. He was amused that the priest thought he could be seduced by the secrets of a primitive religion.

❧ · · · ✠ · · · ☙

The weather was cooler in the swamp today than was normal, Wer thought, perhaps that was why he felt a shiver as Emel, Marta and he neared Jerdon's hut for a meeting with Mathis and Jerdon. The two men greeted them from the doorway and then moved for them to enter.

Wer sat, his mind wandering to more than the weather. Two weeks had passed since Kara and Stephen had married; Wer couldn't decide if they had been the longest or the shortest two weeks of his life as he tried to bring his attention back to the meeting. He forced himself to listen to what his uncle was saying.

"Tomorrow," Mathis was saying, "the ship from Earth will arrive, bringing more military, as well as, priest sent from Earth to establish churches on Theta. I've got my network of priest firmly in place, so we should get news rapidly from that group."

Jerdon added, "We're getting daily news from the villages. We can only at this point put our hope in Stephen and pray he can convince his grandfather to listen to the plan we are proposing to correct the situation here." He looked at Wer. "Have the three of you heard anything from Kara or Stephen?"

Wer gave a swift look to Emel and Marta before saying, "Yes, Emel received a message from Stephen that his grandfather had read the report that included most of the facts about what has been going on here, as well as, Stephen's suggestion that a new treaty would solve most of the problems on Theta. He has told Stephen that he is considering the suggestion, but wants to get information from this Federation Commander Yin-Sing he's sending."

Emel then said, "Stephen seems fairly confident that we can deal with this guy Yin-Sing. He says the guy is hard but dedicated to the Federation and says he digs hard for the truth of a thing. Stephen also said that Kara sends her love to everyone."

As soon as Emel started his last sentence, he focused his eyes on Wer. The three of them mind-spoke all the time with Stephen and Kara, but Wer frequently withdrew if things became personal. Wer knew his withdrawals bothered Emel.

"Maybe you and I should talk later." Wer spoke silently to Emel. Then he spoke aloud to the room.

"I guess we're as ready as we can be. Now, we just have to make sure our people keep the truce and wait for Stephen to make some progress."

Jerdon nodded and replied, "Yes, as ready as we can be. I don't know about you young people, but Mathis and I are hungry and about to have lunch. You're welcome to join us."

"Thanks," Marta said. "If I'd known, I wouldn't have started cooking, but our meal should be about done, and Wer was eating with us."

Wer was relieved when they left, and then Emel told Marta that they were going for a walk while she finished getting their meal ready.

A little way from the village, Emel said, "Well, should we just talk out loud like we were just two men talking about women?"

Wer laughed and felt instantly happier.

"Well, since we are just two men who are about to talk about women, I guess we should just talk."

৩০ · · · ⊠ · · · ৯১

The next afternoon, Haley met Yen-Sing and Bishop Harrold at the landing pad. He would drive the two of them back to the base in a land-rover with Yen-Sing's two hundred soldiers and Harrold's hundred priests following in haulers, and if Hsit came through with his promise, it would be an eventful ride. He had furnished Hsit with the longest range rapid-fire weapons available, and his and Hsit's plans were for hit-and-run attacks on Earth personnel that would be blamed on the rebels and end the truce.

They were thirteen miles away from the landing pad, just reaching Olhair's Valley, when the snipers attacked. Haley swerved and braked roughly, slinging Bishop Harrold to the floor. Yen-Sing had hit the ground before the transport was completely stopped and was already running back to the haulers shouting orders to his men; Haley followed. Weapons ready, soldiers jumped from the haulers and spread out in the surrounding area. The firing had already ceased.

The soldiers returned; they had found no trace of their

attackers. Haley had not expected them to.

Yen-Sing walked the dirt road, moving from hauler to hauler, looking at the carnage. In all, twenty-three priests were dead and fourteen more wounded, some seriously. Yen-Sing had lost thirty-one of his men and had another twenty-six wounded.

"I thought you said there was a truce," Yen-Sing said to Haley.

"Commander McNamara called a truce and, I'm sure, will want to offer immunity for this action, also," Haley said. He knew he was on dangerous ground criticizing his commanding officer, but he needed Yen-Sing firmly on his side before they arrived at the base. "His wife is Thetan, sir."

Haley watched Yen-Sing's eyes closely while he spoke and saw the Commander's pupils slightly contract when he mentioned Stephen. Well, that answered the question of where Yen-Sing's loyalties were, Haley thought. He would have to be very cautious in his disloyalty to young McNamara around the Federation Commander.

Thy sorrow I will greatly multiply
By thy Conception; Children thou shalt bring
In sorrow forth,

John Milton, *Paradise Lost*

CHAPTER FIFTEEN

"No, Federation Commander Yen-Sing," Stephen said. "I will not authorize any use of force against the Thetans until we have identified the group responsible for the attacks on our personnel during the past three weeks."

Yen-Sing, the cold gray office walls behind him, sat across the desk from Stephen.

"Commander," Yen-Sing said, sounding cold and uncaring to Stephen, "regardless of who is involved, we can't afford to lose any more personnel or equipment. Unfortunately, in military actions the innocent are often punished with the guilty."

"The Thetans will soon have the situation under control," Stephen said to Yen-Sing and then mind-spoke to Wer, "Wer, do you have any information yet?"

"Sir," Yen-Sing said, "I have written orders from the Premier which authorize me to take whatever military action I deem necessary to end hostilities and return grain production to quota."

Stephen felt a second of near panic; he knew what kind of military action Yen-Sing was capable of implementing. He had spent a great deal of his youth in training with the Federation Commander.

"Mathis and Jerdon are certain that Hsit is behind the attacks" came Wer's mind-voice, "but even though they can each sense an unusual feeling of confidence, they can't sense his reason for feeling such confidence or what it pertains to."

"Those orders assumed my continued absence," Stephen said aloud. "I suggest, Commander, that you bring in High-Priest Hsit for questioning," he said to Yen-Sing. "Wer, can the five of us join and enter Hsit's mind?"

"You have reason to suspect the High-Priest, Sir?" asked Yen-Sing.

"We'll have to try," Wer answered.

"Yes," Stephen said to Yen-Sing, "I have a reason."

"All right, Commander," Yen-Sing said. "We'll do it your way for four weeks, but if we have not been able to stop the attacks by the end of that time period, I will contact the Premier and request official command of Theta."

Stephen felt immediately less tense; he knew Yen-Sing would keep his word. So, he had four weeks. That was four weeks more than he had at the beginning of this conversation.

After Yen-Sing left, Stephen leaned back in his chair to totally concentrate on his link with Wer. The other three joined the link, and Marta asked, "Can you sense our child?"

Emel's mental laughter rippled through the linked minds. "We only sensed our child's presence moments ago," he mind-spoke. "If you search you can sense the beginnings of life; we think it's about ten days old, so, it may be difficult to get Marta's full concentration." Stephen felt, shared the joy, felt Kara's and Wer's sharing.

"Don't worry about me," Marta responded. "I want things settled so I can go home to have my baby."

"Then let's see what we can find out from Hsit." Stephen thought.

Joined, their minds sought Hsit's mental pattern, and for the first time Stephen experienced meeting a fully shielded mind. They put the full force of their united strength against Hsit's shield and felt his shield strengthen in response to their attack. They kept their pressure on his shield.

Finally, they felt cracks in Hsit's shield, reached through the cracks for images, thoughts, feelings, or whatever they could get a hold on. They had thoughts of power, and feelings of contempt toward the people he would rule, and finally a part of the conversation with Haley before Hsit's sub-conscious warning or fear gave him the strength to close and hold his shield against them. But, all he would know was that someone strong in the power had tried to breach his shield;

they thought he would suspect Mathis.

Exhausted, they broke their link. Stephen had no proof to give Yen-Sing, but he knew now that Haley was also involved in the attacks, and guilty of treason. Now, he just had to prove it to Yen-Sing's satisfaction.

While he waited for Haley to arrive, Yen-Sing finished reading the report from Lt. Gordon, his assistant, covering his observations of the officers under Stephen. Gordon had briefly spoken to him two days earlier mentioning that his conclusion was that there were enemies to the next Premier among his officers, mostly instigated by one man. Gordon's report provided the evidence. But, the evidence was subtle, and there was nothing that Yen-Sing read which would allow him to bring charges.

Other things besides Gordon's report had brought Yen-Sing to the conclusion that Haley was guilty. He just wasn't sure of what, yet. But, when he had interviewed Hsit at Stephen's request, Hsit had used Haley's name like it offered him some type of protection. Yin-Sing had known too many men like Hsit to doubt that he was a dangerous and conniving man.

The most important thing that had brought Yin-Sing to his conclusion was Stephen's suggestion a week ago that he investigate Haley. Since Stephen had also been the one to suggest he talk to Hsit, he was fairly sure that Stephen had information that he wasn't sharing totally. He wondered if Stephen doubted him or for some reason feared for his wife if he confided all he knew.

Haley stepped into the room, saluted, then stood at rigid attention. Yin-Sing studied him in silence and saw a thin sheen of sweat appear on his forehead, but he also saw the hard look in Haley's eyes. Yin-Sing knew Haley would be a tough man to break, but he intended to do so and get to the bottom of things here on Theta before he left Stephen here alone again.

"Colonel," he nodded curtly at Haley and spoke as curtly. "Take a seat."

Yin-Sing saw a slight stiffening of Haley's spine as he sat in the single wooden chair; few even highly trained people would have seen that slight movement. "Welcome to my parlor, Colonel," Yin-Sing thought silently, feeling very akin to the legendary spider.

ဇ · · · ✠ · · · ౿

Haley waited in anxiety for Hsit. He knew that Yin-Sing was dangerously close to suspecting him of some connection to the latest trouble. While Yin-Sing had been interrogating him yesterday, he had sensed his own danger. He knew his next move was all that could save him, and he knew he was going to have to take great care matching wits with Yin-Sing.

He heard Hsit drawing near the clearing, and quickly went over the persuasion points he planned to use to convince Hsit to carry out his plan for the assassination of the future Premier and his Thetan tramp. It had been that weak boy's failure that had put him in this dangerous situation, Haley seethed to himself.

He saw Hsit ride into the clearing and heard him speak immediately, "Colonel, I don't think we should be meeting right now. Federation Commander Yin-Sing was decidedly suspicious when I spoke with him," Hsit said.

"That's exactly what we need to discuss," Haley replied, and continued. "Time is running out, so we need to make our final move and bring this situation to a close. The Federation Commander is hardcore military and totally dedicated to the Federation. If Stephen McNamara and his rebel wife are eliminated, seemingly by the rebels, Yin-Sing will totally crush the rebellion and go back to the status quo. You'll be head of the church, and I'll be Planetary Commander."

Hsit dismounted and said, "Then, let's make our plans. We're too deep into this to not do whatever it takes to be successful."

"No rules in your church against cold-blooded murder?" Haley asked in a mocking voice.

Kara sat in the over-stuffed chair in the quarters she shared with Stephen. The month that Yen-Sing had given Stephen before he contacted the Premier was up, and the hit-and-run attacks had not stopped. Kara knew that Stephen was worried about Yen-Sing taking command, and what would happen to the Thetans under the Federation Commander's rule. She had no doubt that the Premier, the man she knew only through Stephen's memories, would not hesitate to take command away from his grandson if he thought Yen-Sing could get grain shipments going again.

Of course, she, Stephen, Wer, Marta, and Emel all realized that something drastic must be done because the temporary peace on Theta was rapidly deteriorating. Over two hundred of the rebels had left the swamp even though Mathis, Jerdon, and Wer had pleaded with the rebels to remain hidden. The return of the two hundred had resulted in open hostilities in the villages, neighbor fighting neighbor, families torn apart, church men ostracizing the new non-believers, the disillusioned vandalizing chapels.

The story was almost the same among the Earthmen. Work at the fields and the packaging plant had shut down, and the men, under the constant threat of sniper attacks, had too much idle time on their hands. Arguments among the military personnel were a daily fact of life now, especially between Yen-Sing's troops and the permanent force. The priests from Earth were being confined to the base until the threat of hit-and-run attacks had been eliminated, and they were beginning to show signs of strain, arguing among themselves over petty matters and constantly complaining about living conditions on the crowded base.

Kara's mind was seeking Stephen's to share her discovery that Marta and Emel were not the only ones with a child on the way. This morning, she had sensed the growing life she carried.

"Stephen," she called, her mind-speech a mind-shout, "I'm carrying our child." She felt Stephen's shock, his fear, and his excitement.

"Are you sure?"

"Follow my thoughts," she said. "Can you feel the child's presence?"

She felt his connection with the developing, still instinctual, life inside her. Then she linked with Marta, Emel, and Wer who, drawn by the intense emotions they were transmitting, had joined them to find out the cause.

"Kara, I'm so happy for you," Marta sent, and Kara felt Wer's withdrawal from the link, and felt Stephen's pain at Wer's withdrawal as sharply as she felt her own.

"Wer's happy for you both," Emel thought, more to Stephen than to her. Then Marta and Emel withdrew, leaving Kara and Stephen their privacy.

"I want to come to you now," Stephen sent, "but Yen-Sing will be here in a moment."

"I'm fine," she sent and broke the direct link so that Stephen could talk with Yen-Sing undistracted.

Kara tried to quit thinking about all of the negative things and concentrate on her coming child. But the child would need a safe world to grow up in, and the later thoughts led back to the earlier ones.

So   ·   ·   ·   ◼   ·   ·   ·   ⋘

Jason McNamara expected to receive during the coming

transmission a request from Yen-Sing for Planetary control of Theta. McNamara knew he would grant the request and further alienate his grandson. He wanted to send for the boy and his new wife, but the circumstances would make it look as if Stephen were being called home because he was incapable of handling planetary authority.

Five minutes later, he took his place in the transmission-screen chair.

"Sir, Commander Yen-Sing has requested this transmission and is standing by. Before I put him on, I will give you my report," Stephen said.

McNamara listened to Stephen explain the events of the recent attacks on personnel and equipment and give his suggestion that the Thetans he had been negotiating with be given more time to end the hostilities themselves.

"No, Commander," McNamara replied to his grandson's image, "grain shipments must be resumed at once. Already, Earth faces food shortages in the coming year. Put Commander Yen-Sing on."

"Yes, sir, but first I would like to tell you my personal news. Kara and I are expecting a child. You will soon be a great-grandfather."

McNamara sat speechless, something he couldn't remember ever having happen to him before. He needed time to think. His response to Stephen's news could be critical to his relationship with his grandson and to the future of his great-grandchild. Finally, he said, "Congratulations, Stephen. I will want to speak with you again after I've talked with Commander Yen-Sing. Please stand by."

"Yes, sir," Stephen said, and then his image disappeared from the screen.

When Yen-Sing was on visual, McNamara officially gave him planetary control and authorized him to implement whatever measures he deemed necessary to subdue the locals and get grain shipments back on schedule. McNamara concluded his talk with Yen-Sing by saying, "A ship with reinforcements will depart from Earth day after tomorrow. Until that ship arrives, Commander, I want my grandson and his wife protected around the clock."

"Yes, sir. My first duty has always been the protection of the McNamara line." Yen-Sing replied and then relinquished the chair to Stephen.

"Stephen," McNamara said as soon as Stephen's image appeared on the screen, "you and your wife will prepare to return home on the ship that is bringing reinforcements. I cannot have my future great-grandchild endangered."

"I'm sorry, sir," Stephen said, the image of his eyes reflecting a cold determination, "but we will not leave Theta until Kara's people are safe."

McNamara, studying his grandson's face, realized that Stephen might disappear with his wife and unborn child back into the Thetan swamp if he were pushed too hard.

"All right, Stephen," he said. "I understand your concern about the planet under your charge and for your wife's people. I'll talk to Yen-Sing again and have him consult you on any actions taken before I can get there. I'll be arriving on the ship bringing the reinforcements."

He saw the surprise register on Stephen's face. He was almost as surprised as Stephen over his decision to travel to Theta; he had rarely left Earth during the last thirty years. But right now, preserving the McNamara line was more important to him than any of the other problems the Federation faced.

Wer and his uncle walked towards Jerdon's hut. During the past few weeks, his long talks with Mathis about everything from swamp flora to psychic research to the gods had helped to ease his pain over losing Kara to Stephen.

When they entered Jerdon's hut, Wer said, "The hit-and-run attacks have increased. In the last few days, another eighteen of Stephen's people have been killed. We're fairly sure that Colonel Haley and Hsit are behind the attacks. We think that whatever goals they hope to accomplish will have to have occurred before the Premier arrives next week."

"We who, Wer?" his uncle asked. "You said we're fairly sure. Also, how are you getting all the information you keep giving us? You know things that happen at the base almost as soon as they happen."

Wer looked at his uncle's questioning face, looked at Jerdon, and saw the same look on his face.

"I would like to hear the answers to Mathis's questions myself," Jerdon told him.

"Could I have a few minutes to think?" Wer asked quietly, closing his eyes to concentrate on his link with the others.

They all agreed it was time to tell someone what was happening between them,

"Jerdon and Mathis probably could give us more understanding of what's happening to us. Just get their word they won't tell anyone else without our permission," Emel mind spoke before they broke the link.

Wer told Jerdon and his uncle about the mind-meld and the resulting mind-speech, relieved to share his experience with someone outside the group that now shared his mind. When he finished, Wer watched his uncle cross Jerdon's hut in two long strides, then take two strides back to where he had stood.

"Now, now it happens!" Mathis finally said. "Church researchers have been waiting for developments in the telepathic field. All of our research indicated that telepathy had not made the advances that the other fields had, so we were watching for something. But, no one expected anything like what you say the five of you experienced. Can you do this mind-speech any time you want to?"

"Yes."

"How much detailed information can you send or receive?" Jerdon asked.

"It's just like talking, but the receiver knows all the thoughts and emotions behind the words."

"Can you hear other people's thoughts in words?" Mathis asked.

Wer hesitated; he wasn't sure how to explain the experience

they had had trying to break into Hsit's shielded mind. Finally, he said, "I don't really know. The five of us together got through Hsit's shield and picked up images of his thoughts, but other than that, we've never tried."

"Would you be willing to participate in some experiments later?" his uncle asked.

"Yes, I would," Wer answered, "and I'm sure the others will agree."

"All right," Jerdon said, "back to the matter at hand. Can you five try to get into Hsit's mind again or into Haley's? We need to know what they're planning and what they hope to accomplish."

"We'll try," Wer said, and sitting on Jerdon's floor, let his mind link with the other four.

Together they sought Haley's mental pattern among the hundreds of other unfamiliar mental patterns at the base. Stephen signaled his recognition of Haley's pattern the instant they touched it. They could pick up feelings and images, but, as with Hsit, no verbalized thoughts. They sensed his scorn for Stephen, his feelings of impending danger, and his hatred of Kara. They broke the connection with Haley.

"Stephen," Wer mind-spoke, "I think you and Kara should come back to the swamp until your grandfather arrives."

"I have to stay," Stephen answered, "but I think Kara should leave. I had no idea Haley hated her so. He's a dangerous man."

"I'm not going without you," Kara joined in.

"Wer and I will come for you," Emel thought directly to Kara.

"Yen-Sing is guarding us like a protective mother," Stephen sent. "He'd never let either one of you get close to us."

"I'll send someone," Wer spoke.

After the five-way link was broken, Wer told Mathis and Jerdon of Kara's danger.

"We'll send Mellow." Mathis said. "Not even Yen-Sing could look at Mellow's jovial, cowardly face and perceive him as a threat. We'll think up some religious rite for them to say she needs to perform which will allow her and Mellow to leave the base."

Wer said, "I'll wait with horses on the side of the plateau."

While yet we live, scarce one short hour perhaps,
Between us two let there be peace,

John Milton, Paradise Lost

CHAPTER SIXTEEN

Haley watched the round-shaped priest go into Stephen's quarters and trembled in irritated rage. It was almost time for Hsit's man, the fanatic who would die for his gods, to arrive. When he had known Yin-Sing was suspicious of him and learned the Premier was on his way, Haley had known he would have to have Stephen and the savage girl who carried his child killed and the deaths blamed on the rebels. If he did not, Stephen would convince the Premier to have everything that had happened on Theta investigated as his grandson desired, and Yin-Sing would back Stephen. Today was the day, and that stupid priest might ruin the whole plan.

Earlier, Haley had given the order for all ground transport

vehicles to be brought to this area and washed. He spotted Hsit's man wearing the private's uniform he had provided. The would-be assassin went to one of the vehicles and started cleaning, never taking his eyes from Stephen's door. Haley, sweating, every muscle in his body tense, also watched the door.

Finally, Haley saw the door open, and the overweight priest walked out first, blocking the assassin from a clear shot at Stephen or his wife. The fat fool was going to ruin everything, Haley fumed to himself, and then saw the priest walk far enough to the left to be out of the line of fire.

A blaster fired, and Haley watched Stephen stagger, a bloody hole visible in his chest, and then fall. He heard the girl scream Stephen's name and saw Yin-Sing running out of his office.The blaster fired again, and Haley swore out loud when he saw the priest jerk the girl out of the line of fire and start running.

Haley saw that the assassin wouldn't have time to take aim at the girl again. Three soldiers were already almost close enough to wrest the gun from him. Haley raised his own blaster and fired, blowing a hole in the center of the assassin's forehead.

He started running as fast as he could after the girl to finish the job himself.

                 ✺   ·   ·   ·   ✾   ·   ·   ·   ✺

"Run, Kara!" Stephen screamed inside her head. She

staggered behind Mellow who was gripping her wrist tightly and pulling her with him as fast as his unexercised body would let him run.

"Stephen," she cried, holding desperately to his mental pattern becoming incoherent now.

"Hurry, girl," said a panting Mellow. "I'm scared half to death. I'll probably run off and leave you if anyone gets close."

"Stephen," Kara screamed his name. He was there, so were Wer, Emel, and Marta, all trying to give Stephen strength, and all urging her to run. "Stephen," she called his name again.

"I'm here," Stephen spoke, his mind-voice weak. "I love you, Kara."

She saw Yen-Sing face briefly in Stephen's mind and understood the Federation Commander was rushing to Stephen's aide.

She could feel Stephen's love for her, see the way he saw her, feel his desire to hold her again. Then she could feel nothing, she reached frantically, trying to catch hold of his pattern . . . gone . . . nothingness.

She could hear her mind screaming and feel the other three trying to comfort her while suffering their own mental shock caused by sharing Stephen's death.

"Look, Kara," she heard Mellow say, "Isn't that your horse?"

She looked around, found herself just outside the base, and saw Shade kicking down the side of the corral Stephen had ordered built for him. She ran for Shade, Mellow still holding her wrist.

She opened the gate and grabbed Shade's mane. Mellow let go so that she could swing up on Shade's back. She turned back to tell Mellow she would help him up once she mounted, and saw Colonel Haley raising his blaster, his eyes meeting hers. She saw his hand jerk with the gun's recoil, saw Mellow's frightened face swing in front of hers, and then felt the force of Mellow's body slammed into hers from the beam's impact.

"Go," he said, then slid to the ground.

She swung up onto Shade, and the horse leapt into the air, his hooves striking the ground at a full run. The next blaster beam came close enough to singe her arm, but the pain wasn't strong enough to quiet the screaming in her mind. Then she was on the side of the plateau, and Wer was in sight.

Wer, running his horse as fast as it could go, was half way up the side of the plateau when he saw Kara and Shade come over the top, flying toward him like the wind. He kept his horse racing upward toward her until Shade flew past; then, he slowed his horse and spun around to follow, keeping himself between Kara and any who might pursue her.

Kara and Shade where only about twenty feet from the first cover of the swamp when Wer heard a hovercraft come over the plateau and start descending in their direction. He pulled his horse even closer to Shade to protect Kara's back as much as possible. His back muscles tensed in anticipation of fire from the craft. But, even then, he didn't let his link with Marta and Emel drop as the three tried to hold on to Kara's panicked mind.

The cool swamp air hit his skin before he realized he and Kara had made it into the swamp alive. Emel and Marta would reach them soon.

"Kara," he mind spoke, but he felt no awareness back from Kara's mind.

"Kara," he called aloud. "Kara, stop. Think about your child."

He watched Kara pull Shade to a stand-still, slide off to stand on the ground, then turn to look at him. Her face crumpled in grief while tears washed down her face, and a soft keening sound came from her throat. Linked to her mind, seeing her face, and hearing that chilling sound, Wer felt waves of agony. He gasped for breath from the intensity of Kara's pain and leapt from his horse and grabbed her in his arms just as she started to collapse.

Emel and Marta reached them just at that moment, and Emel helped him lower Kara gently to the ground. Wer broke their link.

"Poor Kara," Marta sobbed. "I hope she stays unconscious until we can get her to the village. We've got to hurry there and treat that blast burn before it starts to get bad. Do you think her baby is hurt?" she asked, looking up at Wer.

"Oh, Wer," she sighed when she saw his face, then asked, "Are you going to be alright?"

"I'm fine," Wer said in the hardest voice he had ever heard himself speak. Marta and Emel gave him strange looks, so he softened his voice before saying, "I think the baby is fine. I can still sense the new presence."

Wer swung himself on his horse and said, "Emel, lift Kara up to me and lead Shade."

On the way to the village, Wer stayed silent and shielded. He knew he was traumatized from his link with Stephen through which he had shared all the thoughts and feelings Stephen experiences while dying while sharing Kara's as she watched Stephen fall and felt him die then shared the panic of her flight. They had all jointly felt grief, fear, horror, and a painful urgency to save each other and were all still traumatized.

He was exhausted, but for the first time ever, the only thing he felt at that moment was the desire to kill someone. If he ever found the person responsible for Stephen's death and Kara's unbearable pain, he would rip him apart with his bare hands.

Yin-Sing turned the hovercraft back to base. He watched as Stephen's wife and unborn child disappeared into the swamp. He had briefly considered trying to stop her, but he thought the swamp was probably the safest place for her until he knew for sure that Haley and Hsit had planned Stephen's death. He was going to get the evidence today that would allow him to take the actions necessary to see they were punished.

Right now, he had to send a transmission to the ship bringing the Premier to Theta. He had never imagined that one day he would have to tell Jason McNamara that he had let his only grandson be assassinated and let his granddaughter-in-law disappear with his unborn great-grandson. He landed the craft, disembarked, and headed for the Communications Building.

When he ended the most difficult communication of his life, Yin-Sing sat still for a few minutes and considered the Premier's orders and knew that for the first time in his life he would not carry them out as Jason McNamara expected. His first duty now was to Stephen.

He could still feel his whole body start to shake as he ran from his office to see Stephen falling to the ground, his chest bloody. He had made it to Stephen's side before he died and lifted him into his arms. Stephen was staring blankly, seemingly already lost to awareness; then Stephen had looked directly into his eyes and Yin-Sing had seen the recognition there and the hope. With his last breath, Stephen had said to him, "Save Kara."

Now, Yin-Sing knew he had two tasks to fulfill before the Premier arrived and he had to answer to him. He was going to make sure the girl Stephen had loved was safe and always would be, and he was going to find the people responsible for Stephen's death and kill them himself.

He went to his office where Lt. Gordon awaited him.

"At ease, Lt. Gordon," he immediately said while coming through the door. "I have several tasks to give you that are the most important ones I will ever give you. First, send someone after Colonel Haley. I want to question him now. Send someone else to bring in that High Priest. Put our priest in a lock-down; use some of the Special Forces if you need them to contain the priests. Most importantly, find out where the order to clean vehicles near the Commander's quarters originated and how that uniform got into the hands of an assassin. I expect the trail back to the source of both those things will be as difficult as someone could make it, but I need the answers by morning"

As usual, Lt. Gordon asked no questions. He saluted, said, "Yes Sir," and left.

Yin-Sing sat down at his desk to wait for Haley. He had never felt this distraught in his life, and he knew that what he felt was grief. He was just going to keep the work at hand in the forefront of his mind until a killer was dead and a young woman was safe.

. . . who overcomes
By force, hath overcome but half his foe.

John Milton, Paradise Lost

CHAPTER SEVENTEEN

Jason McNamara sat quietly on the ship's bridge waiting for the next communication from Yin-Sing. He had wanted to kill Yen-Sing with his bare hands when he had first received the communication from Yen-Sing informing him of Stephen's death. The realization that he had lost Stephen had shaken him to the core. He wondered if he been responsible for his grandson's death with his decision to put Stephen in a situation that he hoped would toughen him. If that were true, then he didn't know if he could live with that knowledge.

He was aware that at the moment he was totally incompetent to be the Federation Premier. He knew he couldn't make a rational decision now even if the Federation depended on it, but thankfully, Jackson was handling most things from Earth. He hadn't notified Jackson yet. He wasn't ready. He remembered when his son had been killed. He had been grieved, but he had young Stephen. He had failed the boy, and all his dreams for him were gone. But, hidden somewhere in the great swamp of Theta, a young girl carried Stephen's unborn child, his great-grandchild and heir to the Premiership.

"Premier, sir," He heard Admiral Kay's voice and looked up. "A communication has come through from the Federation Commander. Would you like to receive it in private in my quarters?"

"Yes, Admiral, I would," he said while rising. No one, not even Admiral Kay, knew what information he had received in the last communication from Yin-Sing, and he intended to keep it that way for a while longer.

He followed the Admiral to the office area of his quarters and saw Yin-Sing's face on the screen as he walked into the room. As he sat down in the communication chair, Admiral Kay, still in the passageway, quietly closed the door.

"Commander Yin-Sing, I hope you have something to report on who had my grandson assassinated and information on my great granddaughter-in-law's whereabouts."

"I have the investigation into Commander McNamara's death well underway, and expect to know the names of all the plotters by tomorrow, hopefully, in the early hours of the morning. I've already sent messages to the former High Priest Mathis, who is currently with the rebels in the swamp, to set up a meeting to discuss the safety of Stephen's wife and unborn child. I hope to get word back from him late tonight.

We have the planet under total marshal law at present. Work in the fields and production plants will resume tomorrow."

Looking at Yin-Sing's hard face and listening to his even harder voice, Jason McNamara felt a sense of dread.

"Commander," he said. "I want no force used in dealing with any of the Thetans, especially Stephen's wife, until I arrive. I know better than anyone the importance of the grain shipments, but that can wait until I arrive. I'll be there in four days; just try to capture those guilty of killing Stephen for transport back to Earth so we can have their trials and executions televised. I also want you to be sure Stephen's body stays preserved in that climate for transport back for burial. But most of all, be careful trying to get Kara back. I don't want you to frighten her."

Yin-Sing stared at him silently through the camera for long enough for a few heartbeats before he said, "Theta is under control without violence, and my outreaches to Stephen's wife have been as friendly as I know how to make them, sir."

They ended the communication, but the Premier had noticed the omissions in Yin-Sing's response to him. He supposed Yin-Sing considered those duties to be delegated, so he need make no response.

He had thought about letting Jackson know today that Stephen was dead. Jackson had tried to be both mother and father to Stephen after his parents were killed and loved him like a son, so telling Jackson that the boy was dead would take more strength than even a Premier had on a day like today. He hoped that tomorrow he would have the courage to talk to Jackson.

The next afternoon, Haley waited for Hsit to show up in the same grove where they had previously met. Since Stephen had been eliminated, Hsit had become more of a liability than an asset and would have to be taken care of. Haley would have to use someone else to kill the girl. He could have taken care of her himself if it had not been for that fat priest.

Yen-Sing had been hard to satisfy yesterday when questioning about why he had shot the assassin and then the priest. Haley had stuck to his story that the man had time to fire once more before the three soldiers could have reached him and that he had shot the priest in an attempt to rescue the girl. He had told Yen-Sing the same story, over and over. He hoped his story had finally convinced Yin-Sing through consistent telling.

He saw Hsit approaching and drew his blaster silently from its holster and held it behind his back.

"It's dangerous for us to meet right now unless you think we are in some immediate danger ourselves" Hsit was saying, while Haley pulled his blaster before him and took aim. Hsit's eyes focused on the blaster. "What are you doing?" Hsit asked, his face bewildered.

"You're the only one who knows I had anything to do with Stephen McNamara's death. I just can't risk having you around anymore."

Hsit turned to run. Haley shot him in the back of the head and watched him fall face down in the shady dirt. Haley re-holstered his blaster and turned to stare into Yen-Sing's cold, hard eyes. He recognized the intent and started to considered pulling his blaster from his holster, but he had no time to even finish the thought.

The last thing he saw was the beam from Yin-Sing's blaster flashing toward his eyes.

ൟ   ·   ·   ·   �֍   ·   ·   ·   ൟ

Kara walked slowly and tensely through the mid-day heat toward Jerdon's hut. She could feel the tension around her from the other villagers. The Premier would arrive today, and all of them were tense in anticipation of what he would do when he arrived. She perhaps most of all; she knew he would search the planet for her to take her child. She could see Jason McNamara in her mind from Stephen's memories, and her knees weakened so from the vision that she almost fell.

She neared Jerdon's and became weaker; she now dreaded all meetings with Wer, Emel, and Marta. She knew how concerned they were for her, but she kept her mind shielded, protecting her grief and her guilt. She was so afraid that if they touched her mind with their love and forgiveness that the pain would be more than she could endure. Her actions had led to Stephen's death and a threat to everything else she loved.

She entered Jerdon's hut to the sound of Mathis's voice.

"The disciples and the priests are all sending me information since Hsit's murder, hoping I suppose that we can save them once the Premier arrives. They have managed to undo some of their own damage and repair relationships between the rebels who returned and the Thetans who were against the rebellion. We need to be grateful for that."

Jerdon interrupted, "I think most of those left in the swamp are just waiting to see what the Premier does, and if there isn't any terrible retribution they'll face, they'll go home."

"I'm not leaving the swamp!" Kara felt her heart start to race and Wer's protectiveness enclose her shielded mind at the same time. She felt her heart slow.

"Kara," Jerdon said in a quiet voice, "the six of us in this hut will remain in the swamp until you want to leave. We're a small enough group that even the Thetans who have lived here could never find us if we needed to hide."

Wer spoke equally quietly, "Emel, Marta, and I also share the memories Stephen had of his grandfather. We also have confused emotions about this man, the great love and need to please that Stephen felt, the hurt he felt by his grandfather's disapproval, the fear of the most powerful man in the universe, as well as, our Thetan feelings for a dictator that took over and changed our world."

"I promise you," he continued, "that you will never face Jason McNamara alone unless you tell us you want to face him on your own."

For the first time since Stephen's death, Kara felt a soft smile on her face and said, "I know how much you all care for me. I'm going to be fine and so is my child, so you don't have to keep worrying so much about me."

She watched Wer's face relax for the first time since she had seen him racing his horse up the face of the cliff to rescue her, and gave him a wistful smile. She wondered if things between them would ever be the same after all the pain and worry she had caused him.

＄ · · · ✠ · · · ೞ

By the time the ship had arrived at Theta, Jason McNamara had felt like he was rational, and now he waited calmly for Yin-Sing to arrive at Stephen's office. This little square office would always be Stephen's office to him. He had read Yen-Sing's latest report just hours before disembarking, so he knew Yin-Sing had isolated the Thetan priests and enforced martial law. Civil order had been returned to the local population.

But, while Yin-Sing had mentioned finding those responsible for Stephen's death, there was still no word about his granddaughter-in-law's whereabouts. Yin-Sing had also obviously disobeyed some direct orders, like burying his grandson in a private service on this plant and killing the men responsible for Stephen's death.

But for now, he was eager for Yin-Sing to show up to give his report in person and for them to get started settling the problems on this planet. Mostly, he was eager to find his great-grandson.

He looked up at Yin-Sing as he heard the Federation Commander come through the door.

Emel and Marta calmly sat side-by-side outside their hut in the evening air of the swamp, listening to the now familiar sounds change to night sounds. Emel knew he was finally at peace for the first time since Marta had been so horribly damaged.

"Marta," he spoke mentally to not break the calm of the evening sounds, "are you at peace now?"

"You're a silly man, Emel. You can read my thoughts; don't they seem peaceful?"

He could almost hear a chuckling in her mind; he was momentarily almost overcome by his sudden powerful feeling of love. "You do shield quite a bit. What are those thoughts you hide from me?"

"I suppose if I wanted to share them with you, I wouldn't shield them from you. A girl has to have a little privacy, especially a pregnant girl."

He felt alarmed, "Are you worried about the baby?"

"No, Emel," Marta spoke aloud. "She's fine. Maybe I think about being fat and ugly in front of you. Maybe I worry about you always loving me. I don't want you or Wer and Kara hearing those thoughts."

"She?" Emel spoke with excitment, Marta's real worry temporarily wiped from his mind. "She? You said she. Do you know that the baby is a girl?"

"Yes, Emel, I know."

"That's wonderful! Wonderful! Oh, and you'll never be fat and ugly to me, and I'll always love you. Have you thought about a name for the baby?"

She looked at him with a worried frown on her face before saying, "I had thought, if it didn't bother you, that we would name her Lela."

Emel felt his eyes water while he answered, "I think that would be a great honor to both of them, my sister and my daughter. Thank you, Marta."

She leaned gently against him and asked, "Do you feel lonely now with Stephen gone and Kara and Wer both shielding from us?"

Yes, Emel thought, but he didn't let Marta catch that thought. Life was just beginning to be a little bit normal for them both. The Premier had been on Theta for three months and things were going well. He had even been able to get his parents and bring them to Lela's grave. He did constantly miss Stephen, Kara, and Wer being near in his mind - lonely. Marta had used the right word.

"No, Marta," he said. "How could I be lonely with you here? But, don't worry about Kara and Wer; they'll be fine."

"What do you think will happen between them now?"

"How could I possibly know that? Just sit back in my arms and let's enjoy the evening."

Wer leaned against the corral and watched Kara brush Shade's coat. It had been three months since he had brought her back to the swamp, and the haunted look that had been in her eyes since her return, even when she smiled, was finally gone, but her mental shield still blocked Emel, Marta, and him from any mind-speech with her. He could still feel her grief through the shield.

"Are you going to speak or just stand there watching me?" she asked.

"Why don't we talk?" he asked using the same teasing tone she had used, hoping she would finally talk openly about her pain.

She stopped brushing Shade and gave Wer a serious look.

"With just the six of us here now, the swamp seems lonely, doesn't it?"

With Kara here, Wer would not have been lonely even if Emel, Marta, Jerdon, and his uncle had not also remained until she was ready to leave, but he knew she would feel lonely right now even if a hundred people had stayed. "Yes, it's lonely," he said.

"I keep thinking about my first attack on the base. I thought if we could drive the Seraphs away everything would be the way it had been before they came, but all I did was destroy our whole way of life."

"No," he said. "You were just the first one to take some action; it could have easily been Emel or someone else. Our old ways were doomed the day the first ship from Earth arrived."

"What do you think will happen now?" she asked.

"I don't know."

"I'm afraid," she said, and her shield dissolved.

He went to her and held her in his arms while his mind joined with hers. He felt Emel and Marta briefly touch his mind in response to his joining with Kara and quickly back away and shield. For the first time, he could feel and understand the love that Kara had always had for him, the truth and the strength of her love, and how it differed from the romantic feelings she had for Stephen. He let his mind go so she could see his understanding of her thoughts about Stephen and her deep and strong love for him, her life-long friend.

"I need you, Wer."

"I know."

They stood silently, holding each other in Shade's corral, for several minutes. Wer felt a slight nudge of curiosity against his mind. Startled, he realized it came from Kara's unborn child and Kara realized with him. They both reached out for that touch, but discovered the child's mind shielded from them, two of the strongest telepaths on Theta.

"This could be a bad indication of our parenting ability." Wer said in a joking voice.

Kara laughed out loud, and something deep within her started to heal.

Mathis waited around the breakfast fire with Jerdon, Emel, and Wer for Marta and Kara to come out of their hut and join in the morning meal. Marta had moved in with Kara a few weeks earlier. Mathis understood, even if the younger men did not, that both Marta and Kara were nervous about their pregnancies with no older women around them even if Jerdon had once been a doctor. Finally, amid the smells of cooked eggs, hot bread, and frying meats, Marta and Kara emerged from their hut and walked toward the waiting men.

Mathis listened to Emel and Wer speaking jokingly but cautiously to Kara and Marta and watched Jerdon move closer to the food. He decided that the final planning with the group for Kara's future dealings with Jason McNamara would have to wait until everyone had finished eating.

After everyone had finished eating, Mathis said, "We need to get our plans for meeting with Jason McNamara finalized."

The four pair of young eyes focused on his face, and he continued.

"It helps that you four can communicate directly, but I'm worried about us telling McNamara up front that Kara and Wer plan to marry after her child is born. I'm afraid it may interfere with whatever plans the Premier may have for public displays of Stephen's widow and child to establish the child as his heir."

"It doesn't matter," Kara interrupted. "I'm not leaving Theta without Wer with me."

"I don't think Mathis is suggesting that, Kara." Wer said, looking at her with gentleness.

Mathis suspected that the four of them were probably mind-speaking, but had no way of knowing what they might be saying among themselves.

"I was just saying, Kara, that the Premier may not be easy to deal with, not that you shouldn't marry my nephew," Mathis said calmly. "We need to consider at what point in our negotiations we want to bring that up."

"I'm not negotiable on this. I will tell him as soon as we meet," Kara stared defiantly into his eyes when she spoke.

"Marta and I have discussed this," Emel said. "We are willing to go to Earth with Kara and Wer if that will help. Then if nothing much is said about what everyone's relationship is, we might all just look like Kara's entourage from Theta."

"We certainly might suggest that to the Premier and see if that makes it easier for him." Mathis answered. "Now, are we agreed that Emel will go to arrange a private meeting between the Premier and I in three days from now and agreed on what conditions we will be requesting on behalf of the people of Theta?"

"As long as that doesn't include our former church, sorry Mathis," Marta spoke for the first time. "I don't think I could ever tolerate the group that lied to all of us and then let us be basically enslaved."

"Don't worry about that," Jerdon answered. "The Premier has already abolished the church and put one of the True Churches in every village. Our former Disciples told the Premier everything about the research that has gone on here for hundreds of years and he has taken that part of our church and established it as a Federation Research Organization. It's a good thing we never let them know about what happened between the five of you."

Mathis let his mind wander while the others continued discussing the coming meeting and thought about how different his planet would be from what he had left behind when he finally emerged from the swamp. Oddly, his renewed friendship with Jerdon and his growing love for his nephew eased the pain of the loss of his Gods. But, he couldn't imagine the rest of his life without dedication to something.

"Let's stop planning and enjoy our last three days in the swamp," he finally said.

Four months after his arrival on Theta, Jason McNamara waited alone beside Stephen's grave for the former Thetan High-Priest. Yesterday, a young man named Emel had come to the base and asked to speak to him personally. When the young Thetan had delivered Mathis's request for a meeting and started out, he had turned back and said, "I'm sorry about Stephen, sir. He was a good man and my true friend."

Jason McNamara had been moved at an emotional level he had never felt, a painful longing to know the grandson he had so misjudged, by the young man's words. Now, he looked at the stone that marked his grandson's grave in Olhair's Valley near the swamp's edge. In an oddly sentimental gesture McNamara still did not understand, Yen-Sing had buried Stephen where the boy had first seen Kara. McNamara saw the priest emerge from the swamp and walk towards Stephen's grave. When the man stood before him, McNamara looked into eyes that studied his face in return.

"Your message said you had information about Kara," McNamara said, breaking the silence.

"She's well," Mathis said quietly. "She asked me to tell you that her sympathy has been with you. We're all sorry for your loss."

McNamara nodded his head in recognition of Mathis's sympathy and said, "I want to talk with Kara. Tell her she has nothing to fear from me. She can set whatever conditions she wants for the meeting, and I'll adhere to them."

"She knows that you want to claim your great-grandchild, and she isn't trying to deny you your only family. She and I will meet with you here in one week, under the same condition that you come alone."

"Why a week?" he asked the High-Priest.

"She wanted you to have time to think over her terms for negotiating the futures of Theta and her child.

"Which are?" Mathis asked, remembering the fearless young face seen twice on a transmission screen.

"She wants her child born on Theta. She is willing to grant you authority over the child's education as long as she retains parental authority until the child is at least twelve years old. And if you insist that the child be raised on Earth, she wants to accompany the child with my nephew, Wer."

"Is there more?" McNamara asked, anticipating the years ahead when he could match wits with the girl who sent ultimatums to the Federation Premier.

"All other terms concern the future of Theta," Mathis said.

"I can hardly wait to hear them," he said and saw the evidence of the smile that threatened to destroy the composure of the High-Priest's face. The Premier knew he had finally met his peer, and perhaps for the first time met a man he could call friend.

"We require that Theta join the Federation with the same rights as the other colony planets. We want a treaty that puts us in the same standing as the other colony planets' citizens. Earth will have to trade for our grain, but we will agree to meet your supply demands."

"One of the things all the other's have agreed to is the establishment of the True Church on their planets and a leader, generally referred to as a governor, appointed by the Premier."

"Kara, I'm sure, is not concerned with the former religion on Theta. In fact, I think it will make her happy that the church is gone."

"I don't need a week, then. Tell Kara I'll be here tomorrow," McNamara said, "and that I promise to negotiate terms that will be acceptable to her."

Twenty-four hours later, McNamara faced his grand-daughter-in-law. She was much smaller than he had expected her to be. She introduced him to Wer, the young man at her side, with no other greeting.

"The first thing I want to tell you is that Wer and I will

marry after Stephen's child is born," she said.

"I would never attempt to prevent you from remarrying, Kara."

"I wasn't asking for your permission. And, the terms Mathis told you that I've asked for?" she asked him. She looked him directly in the eyes, and he wondered what she thought of him. Her eyes were hard, but he could see no animosity in them.

"All your terms will be met on the conditions that the former High-Priest," he gestured toward Mathis, "agrees to serve as Head of the True Church and Governor of Theta and that you come and remain at the base until the birth of your child and our departure for Earth. I want to ensure you are safe and receiving the best medical attention possible on this planet."

"Wer and I will be at the base in three days," she said, and, with Wer, started walking back to the swamp.

"Kara," he called after her, and she turned back to face him. "Have you chosen names for the child?"

"I've named him Stephen, for his father."

"What if it's a girl?"

"He's not," she said.

After Kara and Wer left, the Premier turned to Mathis.

"She's very confident that she's going to have a son, isn't she."

"I think you can trust her mother's instinct," he answered, knowing that Kara, Wer, Emel, and Marta had already felt some mind-touch connections with Marta's daughter, to be named Lela, and with Kara's son. Mathis knew the Premier's heir, still unborn, was already the strongest telepath he had ever known about. He wondered briefly what kind of future awaited the Federation under the rule of a telepathic Premier. A telepath already showing a preference for his future step-father, Wer, who was as far philosophically from the long line of Premier's as possible.

"Is she in love with young Wer?" the Premier asked.

"She has always loved him," Mathis said, "but I don't think she will ever be in love with anyone except your grandson."

Mathis could wait no longer to ask the question he had stayed for. "I've been studying the teachings of the True Church," he said, "and talking to one of your priests. The church teaches that only one of the gods of old Earth is the true God."

"That's the basic belief of the True Church."

"Tell me," Mathis asked, the scars on his back throbbing, "do you believe He's real?"

Jason McNamara looked down at the ground that covered his grandson's body. "I hope so," he said softly.

The World was all before them, where to choose
Their place of rest, and Providence their guide:
They hand and hand with wand'ring steps and slow,
Through Eden took their solitary way.

John Milton, Paradise Lost

CHAPTER EIGHTEEN

Jerdon, leaning on his cane, walked slowly through the streets of Visionsite. It had been decades since he had been here as a young priest. The Premier had set up his headquarters here and had, even before his meeting with Kara, set up a hospital with supplies and doctors from Earth for his great-grandson's birth. As soon as they had left the swamp, Mathis, the two young couples, and he had been brought to Visionsite.

He and Mathis had been spending much of their time with the Premier working out the legalities of the new treaty between Theta and Earth and Mathis's new role of Governor of Theta. Today, Mathis had begun his studies as head of the True Church in Theta.

Jerdon wanted no part of the True Church. He knew that Jason McNamara's ancestor had done the same as John Olhair: used the remnants of old Earth religions to make a new church to unify and save to people they were responsible for. He didn't want any affiliation with that church any more than he finally had his own. But, he did understand the necessity of giving the Thetans a religion they could accept as being the one John Olhair had made his church from and, thus, a true one. People needed their gods.

"Jerdon," he heard Kara's voice call. "How did you escape from those secretive and important meetings with the Premier?"

He watched Kara and Marta walk down the street toward him as he answered. "Well, the discussions had turned to the new church, so I took that as my cue to leave."

"I always knew you were a very smart man," Marta said chuckling.

"Is this the way Visionsite looked when you were here as a young man, Jerdon?" Kara asked, her eyes looking around the city.

Jerdon looked closely around him, trying to put words to the changes in the city. "No," he finally said, "it's not the same at all. Oh, the buildings are the same buildings and the roads are in the same places, but the sad decaying look is gone. The rusted areas of buildings made from the old ships have been replaced and glass installed. Things are clean compared to those days. And, of course, the hovercrafts traveling the streets weren't here then. We walked or rode horses everywhere even though we had a few non-working craft left from the ships."

"The main differences," he continued, "are inside the buildings. There's more new material and a lot less dirt, and most importantly, there's climate control. The Premier wants to begin installation of climate control equipment in every building and house on Theta before he leaves."

"Well, I'm not surprised," Kara said, "that he even wants to dictate our housing to us."

"That's really unfair, Kara," Jerdon said. "I think you will be surprised at the things the Premier has suggested for the new treaty that will directly and immediately improve the life of every person on Theta. Maybe, you should try to meet the man half-way. You're going to have to deal with him on a day-to-day basis for a long time once your son is born."

"I know, Jerdon. I really am trying to be fair in my thoughts about him, but then I remember how my mother died, how Marta was raped, and mostly how Stephen always felt unloved. I blame him. But, I am trying to be fair. I'm just not good at it."

"Where's Wer and Emel?" he asked, changing the subject. "You two aren't usually out in town alone with all the soldiers about."

"The Earthmen have built a huge building near the swamp to study the plant and animal life there." Kara laughed out loud while speaking. "Wer thought he and Emel should go and offer to work with them a while to offer their expertise in all things swamp."

"If there is such a thing as a Thetan swamp expert, then Wer would have to be that man." Jerdon said, and he could feel the pride showing on his face. He had raised Wer, and that was the only thing he had ever done that he was truly proud about.

"Yes, I know," Kara said. "I'm really proud of him, too. But, Marta and I are glad to have them out of our hair. You cannot imagine how much trouble two idle men can be for two pregnant women. I was just laughing because we are so happy they have something useful to do besides ask if we need anything."

Jerdon chuckled, "Well, having never been a pregnant young woman, I'll just have to take your word for that and assume that idle young men are a nuisance."

∽ · · · ✖ · · · ∾

"I think I'll go out for a walk and drop by and say hello to my uncle." Wer said while hugging Kara, then turned to the door and started walking away.

She watched him take the first step in horror, then, almost screeching at him, said, "I don't think it's polite on Earth to leave when you have a guest."

Kara saw Wer glance at their guest before he answered. "The Premier is hardly company, Kara. He's Stephen's grandfather and your son's only living relative on his father's side. I'm leaving, of course, so that the two of you can have your first private conversation. It'll be alright, you'll see."

Then he walked out the door, and she slowly turned to face

her unwanted dinner guest.

He looked older than he had in Stephen's memories, and she could see sadness in his eyes that either Stephen had never noticed or that had not been there when Stephen had last seen him. She reached out with her mind and was shocked to find it totally unshielded. She was sure a man who had lived with such power all of his life shielded his mind, even if he didn't know what he was doing. So, she thought, he must be trying to be open with her.

Still just staring at him, she reached into his mind and felt his extreme grief that she knew was for his loss of Stephen. She knew in that moment that Jason McNamara had always loved his grandson and felt the tragedy of his never being able to let Stephen know. She also sensed her grandfather-in-law's honest concern for her child – and oddly for her.

"I think, perhaps, I have been very wrong about what kind of person you are," she said. "I'm sorry. I'm sorry also for my part in causing Stephen's death. I wish I could undo the things I've done."

"It's not your fault, Kara. If we're going to play the blame game, though, my quilt is greater than yours. I approved the original treaty with Theta that drove you to an act of rebellion, and I sent Stephen here at a time that I knew things were bad on Theta. I was trying to make a man out of him when he was already a stronger man than me. I just couldn't see it."

"But," he continued, "neither one of us can change our actions in the past. What we have left is Stephen's memory and his child. I hope you and I can work together to protect both."

Kara felt the tears when they started flowing down her

cheeks. She didn't think she could speak, but she forced herself to utter breathless words. "I did love him madly, you know. I don't know why he had to die, but he'll always be a part of me, of his son, and of Wer, Emel, and Marta. Did Mathis tell you about our connection?"

"He tried to, Kara, but I really can't understand what it is that the five of you could share. I am sincerely glad to know that Stephen shared his mind and his memories with someone else before he died, however."

"I have Stephen's memories of loving you, and he really did love you. He thought he was a disappointment for you."

"If I could change that, Kara, I would, but I will promise you that his son will always know that neither he nor his father could ever disappoint me. That is, if you'll let me be as close to the boy as I want to be."

Kara saw a look in McNamara's eyes that reminded her of animal eyes that were caught in a snare. She tried to make her tone gently humorous when she said, "I think you and I will fight quite often while Stephen, Jr. is growing up, but I think they will be friendly fights with us so evenly matched in our common concern."

She saw the Premier visibly relax before he said, "Maybe one day those fights will become the fights of a grandfather and his true granddaughter. I wish I could thank Stephen for giving me both you and his son."

She understood then what he needed most from her and stepped up to him and embraced him like a granddaughter would embrace her grandfather before she said, "For the first time in a very long time, I think life may work out for me and my people. Thank you."

· · · · ❖ · · · ·

From the warm dark world of his mother's womb, he reached out his mind to the other presence he sometimes sensed reaching toward him. When he touched that other mind, he jerked his mind back, startled by the feminine power he sensed in the touch.

"It's okay."

He heard the words inside his mind. He knew his mother and others could speak in such a way, but this was the first time he had experienced such communication.

"Who are you?" he thought outward.

"My parents are going to name me Lela, after my father's sister who was killed. And you're going to be named Stephen after your father."

"I knew that." He thought back in some irritation. Did she think he didn't know what his mother and the others thought about! Obviously, she was Emel and Marta's child.

"I guess you have all the memories of the five who locked minds, too," she thought. "Do you think we will be the first people to be born having other people's memories in our minds?"

"I think so. But, can't you read the thoughts of other people who come around them, too?" He thought to her.

"No. Can you?"

"Yes, but I can't tell how close they have to be. Do you think we'll be able to talk to them when we're born?"

"No, silly," she thought to him, and he thought he could hear her laughing in his mind. "We won't have trained vocal cords that we can talk with."

He felt her suddenly withdraw from his mind just as he felt the inquisitive pressure from their parents and Wer reach for his mind. He quickly shielded his mind. He didn't know why, but he thought Lela had been right to hide their communication with each other from the others. He had been shielding from Wer and his mother for some time now, thinking it might not be a good thing for them to know how much of the power he had.

He had often wanted to mind-speak to Wer. He knew that Wer would be a father to him and that Wer would be the rock that he would build his own strength on, but he had been hesitant to even talk with Wer until they could see each other. He didn't know why he thought that either.

He felt another mind close by: Yin-Sing. He understood Yin-Sing, and he didn't think anyone else had ever understood this man. He knew of Yin-Sing's commitment to guard him and knew that someday that commitment of Yin-Sing's would save him.

Yin-Sing was often near enough for him to sense and he knew Yin-Sing always watched his mother to protect her from any harm.

He thought then of the times he had been in the mind

of Uncle Mathis. It was the mind of his great-uncle that he thought the most about while waiting to face his life and these people that would share his life.

* · · · ✖ · · · *

Wer felt oddly nervous alone with Kara for the first time since she had agreed to marry him and she had moved in with Marta. But today, the doctors the Premier had brought in from Earth had insisted that Marta go to their hospital and Emel was staying with her, so he had come to stay with Kara.

"You don't have to stay here with me Wer," Kara said. "Of course, it would be nice for me."

"Kara," he thought to her. "It's me, Wer, why are you so nervous? And why am I? We've known each other and cared for each other our whole lives."

"Yes," Kara still spoke aloud. "But, I hadn't been married to someone else our whole lives, and I wasn't carrying another man's child our whole lives. And, now I'm asking you to raise that child and love him like he was your own. I think that puts a little strain on our relationship. Don't you?"

"I will agree," Wer answered aloud, "that you have made my life much more interesting than the lives of most people I know. Let's not be nervous, Kara. I know how you loved Stephen. I understand that romantic part of you that was so attracted to him. I don't believe I ever hoped to have that from you. I don't need that. I just wanted to be the guy you could always depend on, the guy who would always be there to save you, like when I saved you from the rabid dog when you were three. I have always been that guy for you, and I understand the way you love me. We're going to have great lives together, and I will be a good father to young Stephen and to the children we'll have together."

He watched her face change from nervous to comical and listened with his nervousness vanishing as she said, "Well, you just should have said you only wanted to be my hero."

She came into his arms then, just as Jarta, who had arrived in Visionsite the day before, came through the door saying, "Are you two coming, I'm an uncle and I want to go see my niece before all of you go running off to another planet with her."

"The baby hasn't been born, yet. I can sense Marta's labor." Kara answered.

"Okay," Jarta replied grinning, "but let's go. We don't want to miss the whole thing and be the last ones to see her."

Kara suddenly gasped as if in pain, and Wer felt like he was going to faint. While he struggle to stay standing, he heard Kara saying to Jarta, "Sorry, we're too late for that. Lela's already here."

Wer took off with the other two, but with a new worry. He and Emel were probably the first two men to experience the pain of childbirth by sharing the thoughts of a woman delivering a baby. He didn't want Kara going through that, but couldn't figure out anyway he could save her from that experience.

As soon as they got to Marta's room in the small hospital,

Kara hugged Marta and looked longingly at the infant Lela. "She is absolutely the most beautiful little girl in the world, Marta," she said.

"And," Marta answered, "it's not but a few weeks and you'll have the most beautiful little boy in the world."

Just a few weeks, Wer thought. He was really beginning to feel uneasy about the whole childbirth thing. Maybe he should talk to Jerdon. He knew Jerdon had delivered a number of the babies in Quaillian.

Only two weeks had passed when he heard Kara scream for him in the middle of the night. He went running into her room to find her standing with fluid running down her legs to the floor and the crown of the baby's head coming out.

He thought for a moment that he was going to be so panicked that he wasn't going to be able to move. Then he quickly mind-spoke with Emel to let him know what was happening so they could get help while gently lowering Kara to the floor.

"Don't worry, Kara. I've been talking to Jerdon and I can handle this," he said while trying to remember everything Jerdon had told him about delivering a baby.

He had just managed to get his new son in both hands when help arrived. He heard Kara say in his mind, "Seems that you've saved me again, hero."

Of him so lately promis'd to thy aid,
The Woman's seed, obscurely then, foretold,

John Milton, Paradise Lost

PROLOGUE

O n the ship's observation desk, young Stephen, four weeks old, lay comfortably in his step-father's arms. For the moment, sensing Wer's love surrounding him, he felt secure resting there in those strong arms.

The ship rotated, and the receding planet came into view. He watched the planet of his birth shrinking and felt Wer's sadness at leaving behind his home, uncle, and Jerdon.

Even stronger he could feel his mother's fear about going to Earth and what would happen to him there.

"Wer will be fine and so will your mother." He heard Lela say in his mind. The two of them had learned on the day of his birth to shield their mind-speech from the others. "You know you have to go to Earth and learn to be the Premier of the Federation, and you know why."

"You act like you know everything, but you don't," he thought angrily back to her. Sometimes he wished she wasn't coming with him.

Stephen thought about his great-grandfather then and walked in his father's memories through the rooms and halls of the Federation's Government House, a legacy from his father left behind in four other minds. He knew what he needed to learn from his great-grandfather. He understood his purpose and what he had been born to bring about.

With his infant's wail, he loudly screamed his rage against the universe.

About the Author:

Vickie Adair currently lives in San Marcos, Texas with the smartest dog on the planet. She received her Master of Arts degree from SFASU and was a technical writer and university writing instructor for decades until she "retired" at sixty to start publishing all those manuscripts of fiction and poetry that she had been writing and hiding in a drawer.

*Her first published book was an illustrated children's book, **Once Upon A Tooth...a Fairy's Tale**, and her second was a book of poetry, **Sonnet of a Housewife**, and other poems. **Rebels of Theta**, the first novel in the Gods of Arth trilogy, is her first science fiction novel to be published.*

3rd
rd
3c

Third Coast Publishers LLP

For more information and other publications visit:
www.ThirdCoastPublishers.com